About the author

Geoff had a career in the court service, working in county courts, the high court and the court of appeal. He retired in 2017 to pursue his passions of long-distance walking and wood carving. Geoff lost his first wife in 2005, but has two brilliant adult children, a daughter and a son. He has remarried and lives in North London with his wife and her twin sister. 'No Job Too Small' is Geoff's first book and draws on a lifelong interest in folklore and mythology.

NO JOB TOO SMALL

To: Joey, A preocious reader!
Geoff Denman

Geoff Denman

NO JOB TOO SMALL

Vanguard Press

A CIP catalogue record for this title is
available from the British Library.

ISBN 978-1-80016-499-4

*Vanguard Press is an imprint of
Pegasus Elliot Mackenzie Publishers Ltd.*
www.pegasuspublishers.com

First Published in 2023

**Vanguard Press
Sheraton House Castle Park
Cambridge England**

Printed & Bound in Great Britain

Dedication

To Lorraine and Linda, whose old doll's house was
the inspiration for this book.

1. Doll's House

From time to time my wife and her sister indulge in a major clear out of the house. The Covid lockdown had provoked an even more thorough one than usual, during which they came across their old doll's house. It is a rather splendid doll's house, made in the 1960's by Triang, all in wood with steel window frames and even electrical lighting, but it had spent the last half century under beds and on top of wardrobes, and had definitely seen better days. It was consigned to the 'to throw' pile and duly went into the rubbish bin with the old clothes, picture frames, ornaments and the rest. I didn't realise there was a problem until my wife had a bit of a tearful night and confessed, she wished we hadn't thrown it, so in the morning I pulled it out, wiped it down and set about restoring it. It went out to my little workshop and had new hinges fitted, the wiring removed, and a thorough paint job inside and out. I have to admit I quite enjoyed myself, until I went back indoors and found that my wife and her sister (who is also her twin) had decided that the dolls' house was going to a friend in North

Weald who had a young granddaughter, where it would find a good home. That was fine, except that it would now require a full complement of furniture and being ever so thorough they had written a list to help me make it. I was relieved that the list wasn't on a spreadsheet but was horrified at the length of it. Sofa and matching armchairs, bookcase (with books), double bed (with bedding), table and chairs, kitchen units, corner unit and so on. Everything a dolly family could possibly need in fact. I grudgingly accepted the list and went back to my workshop to cut some thin strips of timber and think about making a start. I decided on a wardrobe as a good item to kick off with, as it was quite complicated and would need hinged doors, so I'd soon see if I was up to the task. After an hour or so of splitting miniature wooden doors whilst trying to put hinges on them I decided I wasn't and gave up on it for the day. *I'd look again tomorrow*, I thought.

Next day I went to look at the damage and probably cut up some more timber to start again. I was astonished to find a complete wardrobe, with beautifully hinged doors and daisies carved on the cornice, standing on a business card. It was a smallish business card with tiny print which read:

"Cassivellaunus and Davidillidallion Hollyfoot,

carpenters, joiners and cabinet makers, no job too small.

Domestic and commercial work undertaken."

I turned it over, put it down, picked it up and read it again, but that's what it said. It gave an address which sounded a lot like the summer house at the bottom of my own garden, so I headed down there to take a look and perhaps pay a visit, still totally mystified by the whole business.

Predictably the summer house was there, as usual, but there was nothing else in the least untoward. I sat down on a patio chair and had a think about it. Someone had finished the little wardrobe, really well, and left me their card presumably with the intention of making more items, but that wasn't likely to happen in my summer house.

It was a sunny day, the garden birds were busy, and all the leaves had opened, and I almost dozed off thinking about it. When I glanced back at the summer house there was a foot high, glossy green door in the wall to the left of the actual door, where there had most definitely not been one before. Unthinkingly I got up, knelt down and tapped on the door, which was certainly quite real now. It must have made quite an impression because I remember it in detail, really shiny paint, a brass knocker, and a white painted frame which had somehow melded into the cedar planks of the summer house. The door opened, framing a small figure who I have since come to know as Davidillidallion.

I was quite convinced I was hallucinating or delusional. Here was a flesh and blood man, about a foot tall, standing with his hands on his hips and gazing up at me appraisingly. He was dressed in a mossy green jerkin with a leather belt carrying a leather purse and a knife. He had remarkably long hair and a plaited beard with a bead in, and strikingly wore a long, tasselled red and white striped cap.

I blinked at him, he stared at me, so I broke the silence by holding up the little business card and asking, "Did you leave your card for me?" A slow smile spread across his weathered face, and he nodded and replied.

"That's right, man. Did you like our work? We saw your list of furniture, it's quite a major commission, but we'd be happy to take it on at an agreed, fair price."

His voice was surprisingly deep for such a small person. At first, I thought that calling me 'man' was some sort of hippy style affectation, so I said, "Call me, Geoff, please, 'man' is so 1960's!"

But he just looked puzzled and said, "I've heard your lot called much worse things, I can tell you. Man is what you are, and man is what we call you," so I let the topic go and returned to the subject of furniture, all the time thinking.

"This is unreal and soon I shall wake up and have to attempt to make tiny bunk beds, or else wake up in a straitjacket."

I cleared my throat and asked, "When you say that *you* could take on this work, how many of you are there in my summer house, please?" Davidillidallion replied to the effect that there was himself and his business partner, Cassivellaunus, and that they weren't precisely operating *in* my summer house as such, but simply using it as a doorway into their own workshop, which was vaguely somewhere else. Because they'd left me their business card, he explained, I had been invited to have contact [and commerce] with 'the folk', as he called his kind, and was therefore able to see him and his world.

I nodded, not at all the wiser and not in any way convinced this was real, but I said that I'd consider his kind offer and get back to him soon. I asked if I could find him at the summer house when I did, and he said probably I could, if I came in the right frame of mind and brought the business card with me.

"Thank you, it's been a pleasure to meet you, I hope we can do business soon," I said, a bit formally probably, then walked briskly back up the garden. When I looked back from the kitchen doorstep, the green door might never have been there.

The workshop

2. Cultural issues.

Well, I had a think about it overnight, and decided that, delusional or not, it was worth proceeding so as to get the damned furniture made, so in a quiet moment I wandered back down the garden, sat in the sun and tried to calm my mind. Sure enough, when I looked, the green door was back, so I steeled myself and tapped on the little brass knocker.

Davidillidallion opened the door promptly, and this time I got a look inside, into a dimly lit workshop which was most definitely not the interior of the summer house. There was a work bench in the middle, sawdust and wood chips liberally sprinkled about, and a rack of saws, chisels, drawknives, and other woodworking tools on the wall.

There was also a foot high man much like Davi, but somehow markedly different. This must be Cassivellaunus, I thought. He straightened up from the bench and fixed me with very blue eyes, and we considered one another. Like Davi, he had a long beard with a bead in it, and a long red stripey cap with a tassel, but unlike Davi, he had quite a challenging bearing as he stood , eyeing me up and sticking his thumbs deeper into his belt.

"Good morning," I offered, "you must be Cassivellaunus. I've been talking about some doll's house furniture with your colleague Davidillidallion." He continued eyeing me, so I added, "nice workshop you have, looks like you've got everything you need here."

After another pause, he finally spoke, and said "Davi does sales, but yes, we could take on your commission for the right price."

At least this was progress, so I smiled and said, "Well. I can hardly come in, but could you perhaps come outside, and we could discuss the details?." The three of us ended up on the little veranda of the summer house in the early spring sunshine, and just as a topic to start off our transaction, I asked, "have you been trading from here for long?" Cassivellaunus just looked at me, but Davi quickly replied to the effect that they had traded in the Brent valley all their working lives, but that they'd only recently set up with the summer house as a base of operations.

"Man has been covering all of the Brent valley in concrete over the last years," he said, "so a lot of the folk have moved into urban areas and away from the Brent. Your garden is good for timber, good housing too." I nodded as though I was following this, and said, without any thought, "the

Brent is a mucky little stream anyway, really, especially down near Staples Corner and Brent Cross."

This turned out to be really ill advised. Cassivellaunus stood up slowly and was clearly boiling over. He clenched and unclenched his hands and I found myself wondering how sharp the little knife at his belt was. Very, I suspected.

After a moment he managed to say, "I won't work for anyone who speaks about the elevated one like that. It's sacrilege, plain and simple. Brigantia was here before the road and the shops, and she'll be here when they're dust, praise her. Take your silver and go, man." I was sitting open mouthed and quite confused, really, but Davi was quicker and said, "Its only ignorance Cass, they've forgotten their heritage and they don't live in the world, just in their own inventions. I don't suppose he's got the faintest idea that the Brent has always been sacred to the elevated one, I'll talk to him and I'm sure he'll apologise properly." Cassivellaunus didn't look mollified, but he did give a stiff little bow and stamped back into the workshop.

We sat for a while in silence, then Davi began. "You don't live in the world in the same way that we do," at precisely the same moment as I said, "I'm really sorry—if there's anything I can do." We sat in silence some more, then Davi tried again.

"The folk have lived in this valley and the hills around it since before these islands *were* islands. We've watched it change under the hand of man, slowly at first, but much, much faster in recent days. For us—and this is what you really need to get into your head, the hills, the woods, and especially the river are the same as ever, and the river is particularly important, which is why Cass went off on one. Brigantia was one of the greatest gods in these islands, and the Brent is dedicated to her. It's holy, now, as then. Your own Borough of Brent still has it in its coat of arms! You need to understand that, and show proper respect, and we'll get on fine together. You don't own the world man, you just live here like everyone else."

Quite a speech.

I sat for a while digesting this, then said. "Thank you Davidillidallion, genuinely thank you. You've made the situation very clear to me, and I think I know exactly what I need to do."

I remembered reading about Celtic water offerings, in rivers and at the water's edge, and how weapons, jewellery and other valuables had been ritually sunk, only to be dredged up by archaeologists centuries later. I had decided to make an offering to the Brent, probably down near Brent Cross shopping centre where it's embanked quite close to the access road. I'd drop my offering into the water and ask the river for forgiveness. I was mortified that I'd just discovered these incredible beings at the bottom of my garden, in the best fairy tale tradition, and had immediately succeeded in mortally offending them. I was pressed for an appropriate offering, but thought a two-pound coin would serve, although I was pretty certain it didn't contain any precious metal.

I walked down to Brent Cross, a couple of miles over the hill next to the playing fields, always thronged with crows, and down into what I had never before thought of as the river valley. Over the walkway crossing the North Circular, and so along the embankment of the Brent, noting, with some sadness now, the upturned shopping trolleys poking out of the river. Getting to the actual edge of the Brent was harder than I'd imagined. Clearly it wasn't intended that anyone should get anywhere near it, but I eventually found my way to the water's edge and composed myself.

I had a ritual think along the lines of, "Brigantia, Elevated One, please forgive me for insulting the river Brent, which is yours, and please accept this offering as a mark of my regret and respect," then I dropped the shiny, dense disc into the green water and watched it disappear, doubtless to be dredged up by an archaeologist in due course.

I felt I'd done what I could, so regained the access road and headed home, giving the crows a nod as I passed. I had decided to leave a cooling off period before I approached Cassivellaunus and Davidillidallion to see if our arrangement was still on, so it wasn't until the next morning that I headed down to the summer house. I sat down and waited for the green door to be present again, then tapped politely on the little brass knocker. Davidillidallion answered and seemed quite amiable.

"You've come to talk furniture?" he asked.

I said I had, but that I had also apologised to Brigantia in what I hoped was an appropriate way, and I'd like to tell Cassivellaunus.

"I know," he said, "a bird told me."

"A little bird told you?" I asked, a bit incredulously.

"Big black one, actually," he said.

3. Logistics and finance

I said that I'd like to sit down and talk about how I could pay them, and how soon they could start work, if it was convenient, and Davi said of course—it would be good to firm things up. The wardrobe was a demonstration piece, he said, so that was gratis. I'd had a think about payment methods and decided that the guys probably didn't take BACS payments. Silver or gold were more likely to be the order of the day. I remembered an old solid silver pen I'd kept for years, although it had never worked and likely never would. The Vikings used 'hack silver' which they carried around in the form of arm rings (or more likely as a silver crucifix, no questions asked) and hacked chunks off as required. I wasn't up for that, but I could manage hack*saw* silver, half the pen now and the remainder on completion.

I produced it from my pocket and put it down on the veranda between us, "I hope this is an appropriate form of payment," I said. "I was thinking half now and half on completion. Does that sound acceptable?"

I noticed Davi's eyes had lit up at the sight of the pen, and now he stroked and sniffed it, then said, "Just a moment please, if you don't mind," and shot back through the green door, closing it behind him. I could hear an excited discussion inside and made out the phrase 'half a ton of it' then quieter discussion followed. After a while Davi re-emerged with Cassivellaunus, who nodded and smiled pleasantly at me, which was a relief.

Davi said, "That arrangement sounds ideal and the metal is acceptable, thank you, but could we possibly agree two thirds of the metal now and the remaining third on completion? It will help defray our initial outlay and pay subcontractors."

I said that was acceptable and offered to go to the workshop now and cut up the pen forthwith. A thought occurred to me, and I said, "Could you possibly mark the metal at the point where I should saw it, so that we're agreed on a proper share?"

They looked at each other and Davi went into his workshop to fetch a soft pencil. He went to a point which I'd have said was about two thirds down the pen, then tentatively moved a further couple of millimetres down, and made his mark.

He looked at me a bit defiantly and put the pencil behind his ear, so I said, "I'm perfectly satisfied with that, I'll go and cut up the metal now, and bring two thirds straight back." Deal done!

Back at my workshop a good will gesture occurred to me, so I put the pen in the vice and put a sheet of paper underneath to catch the silver dust from my sawing. I had a feeling Cass and Davi would appreciate every last scrap of silver, somehow. I then cut at Davi's mark, folded up the paper package and headed back to the summer house. Cassivellanus and Davidillidallion were waiting expectantly outside their now totally tangible workshop door. This was clearly important stuff.

"Hello gentlemen," I said, "here is a two third portion of the pen, and here is the silver dust from my sawing, which is of course also rightfully yours."

They were all smiles now and said, "Give us a moment to secure the metal inside, and we'll be happy to plan your commission."

They returned moments later with a brown bottle and three wooden cups about the size of an eggcup.

"We'll drink to a long and happy partnership," said Cassivellaunus, and poured out three cups, one of which he offered me.

"Mead" he said, "the finest old *Cat's Eye* mead, the only proper drink to toast a business relationship."

"Well, Cheers!" I said and tossed the mellow liquid down my throat.

Surprisingly, they responded in kind, with, "Cheers," and a good glug. I'd expected some arcane fairy toast, but never mind. We sat on the veranda of the summer house and talked business.

"We've got stocks of seasoned timber but not enough for the whole commission," said Cassivellaunus. "We'll need to source quite a bit more." He raised an eyebrow at Davi and said "Master Feller Bellerkind?" Davi nodded slowly and replied.

"I think so, he's quick and really skilled, it's just all the other stuff. He does seem a lot better though, and he's had help lately."

"Therapy," said Cassivellaunus.

"Hmmm", nodded Davi, "but Pandemonious Balker used him, and he says it was fine. You just make sure you don't interfere with him while he's working, and pay up promptly, in metal, which won't be a problem on this job."

I followed this with growing interest and asked, "So, this master feller will cut down trees for you?"

I thought Cassivellaunus looked at me a bit pityingly, but he said, "Yes, that's right, we'll saw it into planks and season it so it can be used by the end of the year. There's good sound Ash and Beech for the carcasses, and some nice fruit wood for doors and cornices and detail work."

Half-jokingly I asked, "You won't cut down my little cherry tree, will you? I've only had it three or four years."

"Of course, not," said Cassivellaunus, "there's a much bigger one in the garden two doors down."

I could not tell whether he was joking. "So, can I meet this, Master Feller?" I asked. "He sounds really interesting, And I like working with wood myself, so we'd have something in common." Both of them looked really horrified and shook their heads vigorously.

"Not a good idea, not at all. No, no, no, no, no. He used to have a lot of issues with men," said Davidillidallion.

"He used to eat them," said Cassivellaunus, "he used to be a troll."

We moved on to logistics.

"He'll probably cut most of the timber down at the Welsh Harp reservoir or along the Silk Stream," said Cassivellaunus, "so we'll need some tomte to act as porters and haul it back here. Thorfinn Thorfinnson and his mate would be good."

Davi Nodded agreement, and I asked, "Can you kind of fill me in on what we're talking about as we go along?"

So Davi explained at some length that tomte were pretty much what the English call gnomes, and Norwegians call nisse. Father Christmas apparently started out as a tomte. They attach to a household or area and are very hard working and industrious so long as they're never offended. Davi and Cassivelaunus occasionally used Thorfinn, who was very proud of his Norse ancestry and claimed that his ancestors had come to England with the Great Heathen Army in 865 and tidied up after Ivar the boneless. That would have been interesting work, I thought. His mate Martin was from Hemel Hempstead.

Finally, we came on to 'trim' as they called it. I'd said that the beds would have to have mattresses, pillows and bed linen, and that there would need to be curtains and carpets, so there was much twiddling of beard beads while they thought about who best to approach.

"Catalina and Meg," said Davi eventually. "They are the best, even if they're a bit snooty."

"A bit snooty," said Cassivellaunus.

"They act like they're royalty. Just because they've worked for royalty before." My ears pricked up at this and I asked what the royal connection was.

"They sewed on pearls and did embroidery for your Queen Elizabeth," explained Davi. I was a bit puzzled by this and said I didn't particularly remember the Queen wearing pearl dresses, but Davi said, "no, not this one—the one with the white face and the bad teeth. You know the ermine portrait? They did all those fiddly jewelled bits, apparently."

So, we had a contract, and we had a plan. I would watch with interest.

4. Rollout

Once or twice a week I bake bread. We've come to like it more than the shop stuff, and anyway I enjoy the process. I'll put a bread recipe at the end of this book in case you want to have a go, and I guarantee you'll never look back. I made a small white loaf, and then it occurred to me to make two *very* small white loaves, as a goodwill gesture. I had no idea what Cass and Davi's domestic arrangements were, for all I knew they were shacked up with Catalina and Meg and eking out the proceeds of sewing on Elizabeth's pearls, but a nice loaf never goes amiss.

I wondered down to the summer house with my little loaves in a paper bag and a mellow frame of mind and found the little green door waiting for me. As I approached, it opened, and Davi emerged followed by two characters about his height, but as wide as they were tall. They had exceedingly short legs and enormous knotted hands, which looked very weathered and very strong. The beards and tasselled hats were in the style of those which Cass and Davi wore.

They all stopped in their tracks and stared up at me, then Davi cleared his throat and said, "Gentlemen, this is our client and patron, a man called, Mr Geoff. Man, this is Thorfinn Thorfinnson, and his mate Martin." I knelt so as to be at a better height and gave them a little bow, and said, "it's a pleasure to meet you gentlemen." I'd been doing my homework since my last chat with Davi, and now knew where tomte came from.

Back in the day in ancient Scandinavia, when the founder of a farm died, his spirit attached to the house and the land and protected them. Generations of tomte descended from it, and continued to support and assist the householders, seeking only an occasional bowl of porridge, with a knob of butter, as reward. What the humans of the household must never do, however, was to offer extravagant gifts, particularly new clothes. If they did, the tomte were likely to flounce off and never return, leaving the farm hands to muck out their own stables and fetch their own firewood.

With all this in mind I continued, "I understand that you, Finnbar, are descended from Viking stock, and that your ancestor was a Skeppstomte" (this is a tomte that dedicates himself to ships rather than buildings). He smiled broadly at this and replied, in a voice that came from his hobnailed boots, "that's right, you're very well informed for a man." Buoyed up by this I continued, and said, "and Martin, I understand you're from Hemel Hempstead, a lovely town. Which part are you from?" He seemed pretty happy also and replied that he was from Nash Mills. "Ah." I said, "near the confluence of the rivers Gade and Bulbourne. There have been water mills there since the 1100's, I think."

"That's right"! he said, "my family have served there for centuries. I'll be going back as soon as this job's finished."

"It's been a pleasure to have met you," I said. "I'm making porridge this evening, so I'll be sure to leave a bowl at the back door at dusk, with a knob of butter." There were very broad smiles at this.

"You're a gentleman," said Thorfinn, and they bowed and tramped off into the bamboo thicket, their purses no doubt bulging with my hacksaw silver. I felt that had gone very well. Cassivellaunus must have hauled up at the workshop door while we were talking.

"Nobody likes a smartarse," he said, and went back inside.

"Don't mind him, you did the right thing," said Davi.

"Tomte like their hard work acknowledged, and the only reward they'll accept is porridge with butter. You did well. I think you might have earned a proper name like a real person, man. I'll call you, Mr Geoff."

"Just Geoff would do." I replied, but he looked hard at me and repeated.

"I'll call you, Mr Geoff."

We sat on the veranda listening to Cass sawing and whistling inside, and Davi gave me an update on the furniture project. Thorfinn Thorfinnson and Martin were signed up and had received half payment in advance and would porter the rough logs back to the workshop from the Master Feller's woodland camp, which was somewhere near Welsh Harp reservoir, apparently.

Master Feller Bellerkind himself would always cut timber for silver, and Cassivelaunus had been to talk to him (carefully) and agree a price. He would start cutting in the next few days, so a steady flow of rough timber would start arriving. Cassivellaunus had specified ash, with some cherry and apple for fine work.

"That just leaves the sawpit," said Davi. He looked a bit downcast. "What's the problem with the sawpit, then?" I asked.

"Well," came the reply, "Cass is always top dog and I'm always underdog, which is unfair but it's always how it works out."

"I see," I said, not seeing at all. "Could you not take charge for a change?"

"Wouldn't work," he said, "Cass is stronger, so he takes the top end of the two-handed saw and stands on the ground, I go in the pit and take the bottom end. I get a face full of sawdust on every down stroke. Underdog is the worse job in the whole industry." There wasn't much I could say to that. I could offer to cut the planks with my electric jig saw, but I'd learned by now that when these folk did anything they did it their own way, which was usually the way they'd done it for centuries.

"Well," I said, "this might cheer you up. I've been baking and I've made you a loaf of bread each," and I handed over the paper bag.

Davidillidallion was genuinely pleased by this and went inside to tell Cass, who shortly appeared at the door and said, "The gift of bread is very kind, man, and I apologise for being so rude to you before. If more men took the trouble to find out a little bit about the folk they share the land with, things would be a lot easier." I found out later that bread is a traditional gift to give when attempting to build a relationship with the folk. That was lucky, then. Apparently, it represents something of nature, infused with human effort and transformed, so my bread would seem to fit the bill.

Next day a pit about two feet long and two feet deep appeared at the bottom of the garden, and I made a mental note to think of an excuse for it in case my wife or her sister noticed it. God knows what excuse though. 'Next door's tabby looks a bit peaky and I'm just being prepared for the worse?' No. Some thought required. I waited patiently, sitting at the patio table near the summer house, and in due course Thorfinn and Martin emerged from the bamboo carrying a hefty chunk (for them) of ash, the first consignment of timber destined to become doll's house furniture. They nodded cordially to me—I *had* remembered the porridge thank goodness, and they began a log pile next to the summer house. Another excuse required, for a log pile this time, I thought. A little later Cassivellaunus and Davidillidallion emerged from the green door with tool bags and set up two trestles onto which they manhandled the log. The plan was evidently to split the log with wooden wedges, so they started with a chisel to make an opening then hammered in a wedge with a mallet. After three wedges a split appeared, and the log was on its way to becoming planks. Back into the workshop then, and the lads emerged with a two man saw. Saw pit time had arrived, and I didn't want to embarrass Davidillidallion as he got repeated faces full of sawdust, so I quietly headed back up the garden. It looked like my furniture commission was under way!

Thorfinn and Martin

5. Setbacks and delays

Over the next couple of weeks items of furniture began to appear on my workbench, presumably made using Cassivellaunus and Davidillidallion's stocks of seasoned wood. The newly cut planks of freshly sawn wood were drying out in the summer house, and yet another excuse was required, this time for the neat little stacks of ash and cherry. 'I'm planning to make a model of the Taj Mahal, and it's already been done with matches and with lolly sticks, so I'm using tiny planks of English hardwood... No. Think again.

The finished furniture, so far comprising a dressing table, the original wardrobe of course, and a chest of drawers, was exquisite. The grain was matched across the doors and drawers, the decoration was carved with the sort of precision only little hands could achieve, and every piece had a beautiful beeswax lustre.

My wife had examined them and said, "You're getting really good at this you know. The drawers open and everything, and it looks like it's made with real little carpenter's joints."

"Yes," I replied, "dovetail joints. Very fiddly."

The tissue of lies was getting a bit thin though, and I was feeling increasingly guilty for taking the credit for Cass and Davi's craftsmanship. I'd have to fess up at some point soon, I knew.

Then, towards the end of April, it rained. It rained for day after day and night after night. Predictably, as happened every year, the patio began to flood. First a skim of water over the flagstones, but by morning there were five or six inches of water, spreading over the bottom half of the lawn in an irregular delta and edging up the footings of the summer house. I had always assumed there must be an aquifer or an underground stream which flooded onto the surface after heavy rain.

Our next-door neighbour said he had what he called a spring in one corner of his garden, which never dried out, and was home to frogs and toads. I remembered a few years back when the flood had occurred, and the girls had asked what I was going to do about it. I went out to the workshop and made a little Thames sailing barge, with a handkerchief sail, rigging and everything.

"Look," I said. "Now when it floods, we can go sailing!" They hadn't been impressed. I think they had engineering works and drainage projects in mind.

This year was different. Cass and Davi's front door was not far above the tideline, and where their other dimensional workshop was, gods alone knew. I got my wellies on and waded through the [surprisingly deep] water to the summer house, where I found no green door, no sawpit, indeed no evidence whatsoever of their existence. The weather was not conducive to a meditational mindset, it was still pouring and pitter-pattering in the giant puddle, so I plodded back to the house and awaited developments. I checked again at about nine p.m. and found a sodden and very agitated Davidillidallion near the back door, attempting to shelter under the rim of the bird bath.

This was unsettling, as I had invariably gone to the bottom of the garden to see the little folk (as people have from time immemorial, thinking about it. Fairies at the bottom of the garden and all) so to find Davi here, in the rain, in the dark, seemed quite a big deal.

"Come into the workshop and dry off," I said. "You can tell me all about it. I don't have any mead, but I'll get you an eggcup of port or something." I made up an off the cuff, cock and bull story about going to check that the workshop wasn't leaking, then took Davi inside with a bottle of tawny port and an eggcup and switched on the oil filled radiator. I gave him a hand towel for decency and politely looked away while he took off his soaked clothes. Along the top of the radiator, I lined up a pair of stripey hose, a tiny, holey vest, a mossy coloured jerkin, a shoulder cloak which looked like it was made of moleskin or something similar, the stripey cap with its tassel, a pair of high leather boots, a tiny belt with a purse and a knife, and the loudest red boxer shorts you have ever seen, in a size XXXXS, with a pink heart pattern. Then I poured him an eggcup of port and sat down to hear his tale.

As I had thought, the floodwater had begun to infiltrate their workshop at around midday, and they had sat down and made an action plan, then taken their hand made wooden boat out of storage and launched it onto the flood to be loaded up with tools. They successfully poled their way to the higher ground in the south, unloaded the tools, and headed back for the best quality timber. By the time they got the timber to higher ground it was dusk. They were tired and wet and totally focussed on the task in hand and hadn't given any thought to the risk of the stalking death.

"Um, run that by me again," I said. "The stalking death, in *my* garden?"

Davi held up his hand at me to indicate that I should shut up and hear him out, then explained that they had stashed the tools in their temporary accommodation behind my workshop (I made a mental note to find this later) and had gone back through the rose bed, close to the shrubs that line the fence, to collect the timber.

As they got close, Cassivellaunus stopped dead and hissed, "Freeze", which of course Davidillidallion did. Among the leaves were the huge, yellow, lantern eyes of the stalking death, and they were rivetted on Cass. Very slowly he reached for the axe at his belt and slid the shaft free, then held it out of sight behind his back.

"Go, go now, but carefully," he said, then bellowed at the top of his lungs, "here puss, puss, puss."

"OK, OK," I burst out, "you're telling me that the stalking death is next door's tabby?"

Davi looked at me sadly. "It might be a cuddly family friend to you," he said, "but it's a razor clawed, fanged menace to everything else out there, including us. You ask the Blue Tits. I left my best mate to deal with it on his own, and I don't know if he made it." He hung his head, and I furtively topped up his eggcup.

I told Davi to warm himself up while I went outside to look for Cassivellaunus. I fetched a torch from the house. As an excuse I told my wife that I was checking for leaks in the workshop roof. "You're obsessed with that workshop," she said. I then headed off to the rose bed to search for Cassivellaunus.

The rain had eased but it was fully dark by now. I looked under every bush and behind the greenhouse and everywhere else I could think of where a foot high person might be lying, injured. There was absolutely no sign of him, although I did see next doors tabby sitting in the shelter of the dense old yew, observing my movements. I sincerely hoped she didn't contain Cassivellaunus. Pretty crestfallen, I went back to the workshop to tell Davidillidallion that we'd have to wait until morning to carry out a proper search.

"You should sleep in here tonight," I offered, "I'll leave the radiator on to dry your things, and early tomorrow we'll organise a search, when we can see properly."

As I shut him in, he said, "Thank you, Mr Geoff, I do appreciate it. See you tomorrow." I could have cried.

Flood evacuation

6. Rescue fund

Early next morning I told my wife and her sister that since the rain had stopped, I was going to do my Ba Duan Jin in the garden. I really should have introduced them by now or I'll be at dire risk of referring to them as 'her indoors and her sister'. They are Lorraine and Linda, and they are two of the dearest people in my life. They put up with limitless irritations and are surrounded by my carved stools and treen. 'Stick with me girl and you'll never want for a wooden spoon'. I digress.

I let Davidillidallion out of the workshop and we immediately headed for the rose bed and the shrubs. Next door's tabby was still hanging around, so I shooed her off, and began quartering the bushes, looking for a tiny body, I suppose. Then Davi yelled out that he'd found Cassivellaunus' axe embedded in the trunk of the birch tree. We stood at its base and our eyes traced its trunk upwards.

In the thin, whippy twigs at the top was a little bundle like a bedraggled bird or a piece of windblown litter.

"Cass!" we both said at once. There was no response, so I ran to fetch the step ladder and went to the platform at the very top. By bending the trunk of the birch towards me I could just reach Cassivellaunus, although it occurred to me that if I let go of the tree, he'd be catapulted straight into next door's garden, and the lurking puss. I prized his frozen fingers off of the bark and laid him in my old green hat, with his boots sticking out of one side and his cap tassel hanging out of the other. With the brim folded together the hat made a makeshift stretcher, and I carried him into the workshop and carefully put him down on the bench.

I thought Davi looked a bit distraught and helpless, so I passed him some of the wood I'd cut up for my own attempts at furniture, and said, "Do you think you could get your tools and knock up a cot for Cass, and perhaps cut up that hand towel for a mattress and a bed cover." He pretty quickly had an emergency cot, and we positioned it in the corner behind the oil filled radiator, for a bit of secrecy. Lorraine was unlikely to go to the shed, but she might just want a paintbrush or something. Linda didn't go there. Cass still hadn't shown Any signs of life, he was horribly pale, and his lips and fingers looked blueish. We carefully undressed him and found a long, livid cat scratch from his left knee to his ankle. Davi and I carefully covered him with the towelling, then sat back and looked at him, trying to piece together what had happened.

"When I crept off, the cat had him cornered by the birch tree, but he had his axe ready, and he wasn't giving up," said Davi. "I think he swung at the cat and gave it pause for thought, then whacked his axe into the birch and used it as a step to get to the lowest branches. The cat clearly got its claws into him, but he kept going up until the branches were too thin for the cat to climb. It had him treed though, and hung around till we came looking this morning, so he's been stuck up there all night." He must be hypothermic, I thought, or whatever the little folk equivalent is. I nearly said that we should get him to hospital but thought better of it. It would probably be a sure-fire way to get him scanned, catalogued and dissected. He'd no doubt end up stuffed, in the natural history museum. Davidillidallion had already thought it through, however.

"He needs Old Mother Airmid," he stated. "She's expensive and probably very busy, but she's the best, and I'm not sure his chances are that good unless she tends to him."

He stared at the little pale figure, motionless under the hand towel. "Expensive is not a problem," I said. "I'm more than happy to pay, and I owe it to Cass. He was working on my commission when this happened."

I fetched the remaining third of the pen and sawed it into convenient rings while Davi watched. "Will this be enough though?" I asked.

"Oh yes," he said.

"Thank you so much."

Next door's tabby

Once we'd sorted out payment, Davi said, "I'll call Old Mother Airmid and tell her it's urgent. Do you have something meaty please? I'm sorry to make so many demands, but I don't see any other choice."

"Don't worry at all, Davidillidallion," I said, "I can easily find something."

Luckily, there was leftover chilli in the fridge, so I put some in a takeaway box and took it out to Davi. He drew his belt knife and cut straight twigs from the lilac bush, then went down to the unflooded end of the lawn and started setting them out on the ground. I watched with interest and soon realised he was writing runes. I'd learned the Elder Futhark alphabet when I carved Viking style boxes, and I'd just managed to make out the runes Kenaz, Othala, Mannaz and Ehwaz, which spelled 'come', when Davi finished his message and a large glossy black crow promptly arrived on the lawn. Davi offered it the chilli, which was gratefully accepted, then leaned close to the bird's head and muttered some sort of instructions or message. A crow whisperer, I thought. The bird nodded, blinked and took off in a westward direction, on a dead straight course. As the crow flies, in fact. Now we'd wait for the response, I presumed. I couldn't help thinking of Odin's ravens, Huginn and Muninn, who acted as his scouts and his spies. Of course, Odin discovered the secret of the runes, after great personal suffering. Could the crow family read runes? I wondered, or had they just come to associate patterns of twigs with chilli con carne? Likely to remain a great unsolved mystery. In any event the crow was back within the hour and told Davi that Old Mother Airmid would be along this afternoon. Davi paid him off with some kidney beans and rice which he must have reserved from the first bribe, and we settled down to wait.

I'd learned by now that the folk generally assumed that you couldn't see them, which seemed to be the case, except that I'd had some practice. I said to Davi, "I don't want to put Mother Airmid off, I'll keep out of the way while she's here. Just let me know if I can do anything to help."

I settled into a patio chair on the top patio near the house, and put my nose in a book, doing my best impersonation of a totally oblivious human. I could see the whole garden from here, and after a while there was a bustle in the bushes and a very elderly lady, about Davi's size, emerged. She was stooped and very wrinkled and wore a fringed shawl over a patchwork skirt and a bodice made of moleskin. She carried a wicker basket with a cloth over it and a tall staff and peered around myopically as she emerged into the light. She had a certain presence, however. I didn't think next doors tabby would mess with her, somehow. Davi must have been waiting for her and ran down the garden to greet her and show her up to the workshop. She was in there a while. I was bursting to creep over and peek around the door, but I contained myself and carried on impersonating an oblivious human. Eventually they emerged and walked down to the birch tree, where she did a little ritual walk around its trunk, shaking her staff in the air, then faced next door's garden and screamed something which sounded a lot like a curse in Gaelic to me.

That's at least half of your nine lives used up Puss, I thought. She and Davi then got their heads together for a while, after which he gave her a little leather purse and she departed into the bushes from which she'd emerged.

Once everything was quiet, I followed Davi into the workshop and asked how the consultation had gone.

"She says his bones are chilled and he'll take a long time to get properly warm again," he said. "She's left me tea to make up and says as soon as he's awake he should take a cup at dawn, another at noon and a third at dusk. She's also said some healing prayers over him, thanked the spirit of the birch tree, and cursed the stalking death. That's pretty thorough treatment, I'm sure he'll get well soon."

I offered to fetch him our smallest pan to make the tea in, and he said that if I didn't mind, he'd light a small fire to boil it, and to cook. I said so long as it was outside, he'd be welcome to. Now we settled down to wait for Cassivellaunus to come round and drink his tea, hopefully on the road to recovery. I sharpened his little axe for him while we waited. I felt he'd appreciate that somehow.

By that evening Cass was back with us, shivering and chattering his teeth and grateful for the heat of the tea, even though he said it tasted foul. Like frogspawn and mould, he said. *It conceivably is frogspawn and mould*, I thought. Never mind. When he'd settled a little, he confirmed that he had indeed just made it up the tree ahead of puss and couldn't then come down because he could see her prowling around below.

After a couple of hours, he couldn't have come down anyway, he said, because his hands and knees were so cramped. By the time we'd got to him he couldn't feel his hands at all. I said that he should rest, and that I'd make some soft white bread for him tomorrow, then I wished him and Davidillidallion a good night, and headed indoors.

"Mr Geoff," Davi called after me, "you're all right, for a man. Thank you again."

Old Mother Airmid

7. Relocation

After a week or so in my workshop Cassivellaunus was feeling much better. He was up and dressed and soon declared that it was time to migrate north again to his own workshop and get on with the project. I would have worried about the threat of the stalking death, except for the fact that I'd happened to chat with the next-door neighbour over the fence the day before, and he'd been complaining about vet's bills.

"Hundreds of pounds for a few stitches and some antibiotics," he'd moaned, "and now the damned cat won't go out of the house." I didn't think that Mistress Tabby would be a problem somehow.

Cassivellaunus and Davidillidallion headed north down the garden and came back with a little barrow, reporting that the flood had abated, and all was well. I'd kind of noticed this from the kitchen window but didn't comment. They loaded up their tools first and took turns to trundle them through the rose bed, past the birch and down the side of the garden to the bottom patio and the summer house. They were back in due course to collect their best timber, and I couldn't help thinking how much easier it would have been to carry the whole lot for them, but I knew by now it was pointless to offer. By late afternoon they had successfully relocated to their own workshop and were sitting peacefully on the veranda, so I strolled down for a chat, and to talk business.

"Must be good to be back at the old workshop, gentlemen," I said, "I expect you'll be starting up production again soon." Davi nodded and replied, "I think we're ready for some of the big stuff now, Mr Geoff. We've looked at your wife's list and thought we'd tackle the 'kitchen units'. What are they though?" I foresaw a problem here.

"Er, we don't cook on fires like you do," I began.

Only to be interrupted by Cassivellaunus who said, "Yes you do, I've watched you." I took a deep breath and said, "OK, apart from barbeques in the summer, we use electricity, and have cookers, fridges, dishwashers and the rest all built into the kitchen."

Cass smiled pleasantly and replied, "Oh, yes. We have electricity too. Power tools." I think my mouth fell open at this point, because Davi broke in and explained,

"Pandemonious Balker has what you lot call a 'craft multitool'. It can do cutting, routing, polishing, all end of jobs. He has to plug it into a USB socket to charge it though, so he hangs around waiting for men to leave their PC switched on, then charges the tool. Some men leave their PC plugged in all day, even if they're not using it." I had a vision of a gnome using a craft mini tool like a pneumatic drill but shook it out of my head.

"He reckons his workshop is the most modern in the kingdom," said Cass. "He doesn't hold with traditional skills; reckons they're outdated and slow. To be honest its people like him that are destroying the craft."

They sat looking thoughtful, so I tried a different approach and suggested, "Why don't you, Davidillidallion, come up to the house while the girls are out, or busy, and take a look at the kitchen? It will give you an idea. We're just talking little cupboards really, but some of them have to look like cookers or fridges."

They both thought this was a workable approach, so I said I'd pop down the next day when the coast was clear and show Davi around.

In the morning I waited until Lorraine was on the phone and I could hear Linda tapping on the laptop, then went to the summer house and knocked on the door. Davi was ready and waiting, so we headed back to the house. I checked that the coast was still clear, then beckoned him into the kitchen. He stepped over the threshold pretty cautiously, but then looked around and took it in with genuine interest.

"These are the kitchen units," I whispered, "and look, this one is a cooker with an oven here and a hob on top, for cooking on flames, and this one opens and it's a fridge, a cold cupboard for storing food." Then Linda and Lorraine walked into the kitchen together.

They had a twin special power of simultaneously deciding something, without any consultation, and immediately doing it together. They'd used that special power at this particularly inconvenient moment to walk in on us both and announce that they were going to the Co-op up the road.

"Do you want anything?" asked Lorraine.

"No, no I'm fine thanks." I muttered. "Remember your masks." I was scanning the kitchen for Davi but there was neither hide nor hair, so I presumed he was hiding. The girls took the hessian shopping bags from the corner by the door and headed out.

Once the front door closed, I called. "Davidillidallion, are you here?" No reply, so I looked outside, then hurried down to the summer house. Cassivellaunus said he'd thought Davi was with me, and no, he hadn't come back, so I took a seat at the patio table to think about it. He wasn't in any of the cupboards because I'd looked, he wasn't anywhere obvious like under the table or behind the pot plant, but he might, it began to dawn on me slowly, he might very well have dived headlong into the hessian shopping bags which had been right next to him. In which case he would be somewhere in the cereal isle of the local Co-op by now. Too horrifying to think about.

I hung around anxiously till the girls came back, then hurried out to meet them and offered to carry the bags.

"We've carried them all the way from the shops," said Linda, "but thank you."

I hurried into the kitchen ahead of them, and as I'd predicted, Davi clambered out of one of the bags and legged it out of the house and into the shrubbery. I took a deep breath, calmed myself and helped unpack the shopping. When things had settled down, I headed nonchalantly down the garden to sit on the summer house veranda. Lorraine had pointed out that this was becoming habitual lately, and I said it was a very relaxing spot and a good place to meditate, which I have always insisted is a valid lockdown activity.

Davidillidallion appeared in due course, bubbling over with excitement.

"You should see that place, Mr Geoff, it's rammed with everything you could imagine — oats, and peas, and tree sap, and *dreamies* and everything!" 'Tree sap' I thought —ah —maple syrup, of course.

"What *are* Dreamies?" He asked. I answered without sufficient thought that they were cat treats which owners bought to reward their pets. He looked at me pretty hard for a while, so I quickly continued.

"Well, Davidillidallion, I *do* know the place, and if there's anything you'd like or anything you really need, just let me know and I can get it for you and leave it here on the veranda. It would be no trouble; in fact, it would be a pleasure."

A predatory gleam came into his eye, and he said, wistfully, "One of those huge sacks of oats would be marvellous, half a year's supply, and a bottle of tree sap to put on them."

I made a mental note to add large porridge oats and maple syrup to the shopping list, and said, "I'll get those for you, Davi, no trouble."

He beamed up at me and said, "We'll start on the kitchen units tomorrow, Mr Geoff, kitchen units with cookers and built-in fridges and everything. No problem."

As I turned to go a thought came to me, and I asked. "How did you manage to see all this stuff, by the way? Don't tell me you went round the Co-op with your beardie, tasselled head sticking out of Linda's shopping bag, like a chihuahua?." He looked a bit shifty and said that no, there had been a little hole in the bag, just in the right place to look out of.

"OK," I said, and went inside to look. Sure, enough my favourite Eden Project bag, the one with the chillies on, had a triangular cut which looked like a small sharp knife had made it. *Right*, I thought, so we sew that up, and forget all about it. A minor nuisance, but interesting to consider what the lads might be driven to by curiosity.

8. Just call me Cinders.

I had decided it was high time to own up to Lorraine. The incident in the Co-op had been a close call, and there was no guarantee something similar wouldn't happen again. At what I thought was a suitable moment I said, as casually as I could.

"I've been doing some research into the little folk, you know, fairies at the bottom of the garden and all that. You've probably noticed me hanging about down by the summer house, I think it might be on a ley line."

"Oh God, it's like the UFO episode last year," she said. "I remember you out there every night with a pair of binoculars, watching the skies. So long as it doesn't get obsessive, I guess there's no harm in it though, there's not a lot else to do in lockdown after all."

"OK love," I said, "I'm always around if you need me for anything." I felt a lot better for the partial honesty. I really didn't feel ready to say that I was communing with a couple of fairy joiners at the bottom of the garden.

Next time I visited Cassivellaunus and Davidillidallion they both looked grumpy. I resisted making *Snow White* wisecracks and asked what the problem was, and Davi took me aside to explain.

"We have a commission from Grand Duke Ignaceous De Beremond," he said, "and it's becoming a problem."

"I'd have thought working for nobility could only do you good," I said. "You could put 'by appointment' on your business card, and he must pay pretty handsomely." He shook his head sadly.

"No, Mr Geoff, that's part of the problem. For a start he's totally fickle. He originally ordered a luxury chaise longue and we started work, then he decided he needed two, and no sooner had we started on that than he changed his mind and wanted a four-poster bed instead. All the timber we'd already used was pretty much wasted, and we'd spent hours on it."

I thought on this and said that if my project was taking up too much time, it could wait. I couldn't get the furniture to the recipient until after lockdown anyway.

"You're very kind, but that's not all of it." He continued. "His Grace generally forgets to pay our invoice, or if it is paid it's in Fairey gold, which turns to Autumn leaves when you try to spend it. Plus, other tradesfolk get to know that you're working for His Grace for free, assume you're a gullible idiot and try to take advantage."

"So," I said, "it's a lose-lose situation. Why don't you tell him that you can't take his commissions any more, and let him look elsewhere?"

"Because I don't want to wake up to chicken's feet," said Davi flatly.

"Oh, I don't know, I said, "I've had them in China. Don't think I'd want them for breakfast though. The dipping sauce was good." Davi shook his head sadly and explained. "What I mean is that you might wake up and find that your own feet have changed into chicken's feet during the night. You'd have an irrepressible urge to scratch in any dry soil you came across."

"Ah," I said.

He continued. "The grand duke is very old, very powerful and not someone you want to make an enemy of, and we're stuck with him, which is why we're both a bit down."

"Cheer up," I said, "I'm sure there must be a way to get you out of this without anyone getting chicken's feet syndrome. Give me a while to think about it." A rash offer, as it transpired.

A couple of days later Davidillidallion was waiting for me on the verandah, and said he had a proposition I might be interested in. Apparently, there was a ball at the Ducal palace the next evening, on the night of the new moon, and Cass and Davi were invited, along with Catalina and Meg, the seamstresses. All of them worked for His Grace and were therefore on the guest list.

Davi explained that, if Catalina and Meg 'put the glamour' on me as he described it, I could go with them without detection, see the duke and his household and perhaps then formulate a plan to get Cass and Davi out from under their obligations. I wasn't at all sure at first, I wanted to know what 'the glamour' was, how long it lasted, were there side effects etc. Davi reassured me on these issues though and said I should dress as a servant and meet them at the summer house at dusk.

With some trepidation I fished out an old white shirt from my days in the court service and put it on with its wing collar and tabs. A plain black suit and polished shoes, and I *thought* I approximated to what the servant of a fairy carpenter and joiner might look like. Who knows though? As an afterthought I found my little knife with a handle in rowan wood. When I was heavily into wood carving, I'd made this little knife, and I remembered that rowan gives unrivalled protection from witches and the wiles of the little people.

Crofters made crosses of rowan twigs tied with red thread and tied them over the doorway. I slipped the little knife in my pocket, then took a deep breath and headed down the garden to the summer house.

Catalina and Meg had arrived and were waiting with Cass and Davi on the veranda. They were tiny but exquisite, their complexions unblemished and their green dresses floaty and ethereal, as you might expect from two professional seamstresses with centuries of experience between them.

Cass and Davi had brushed up well, Cass in a long bottle green coat with a high collar and white trimmings, with brass buttons up the front. He'd swapped his stripey hose for plain white and wore a black hat with a wide brim and a feather, which reminded me of the English Civil War. Davi was similarly kitted out in a dark brown coat and again a splendid hat, which must have been the accepted formal wear for Ducal balls.

Catalina smiled beatifically at me and said, "So very young and naïve, aren't they? They come and go in less than a century yet think themselves wise."

Meg nodded her agreement and said, "Very sad really, but they do have vigour. This one's put a rowan handled knife in his pocket, so he would seem to understand the fundamentals." They were discussing me in the manner of two maiden aunts watching a new family member playing on the rug, I realised.

Catalina finally turned her attention to me, and half chanted, half asked, "Are you open to the live magic which flows through the worlds? Do you trust me to transform you for this one night of the new moon, and return you to your own kind afterwards?"

"Say, 'I am and I do'," prompted Meg. As I spoke these words, Catalina touched my kneecap (which was the limit of her height) and I felt the world shift around me. I was their size, and the whole world looked different from this perspective. More particularly it *was* different, human artifacts like buildings faded to the status of mere shadows, but the natural world took on a tremendous vibrance all around me.

Mistresses Catalina and Meg

Still stunned by this transformation, I was goggling at everything as we all set off in the general direction of Hampstead. What a bizarre journey it was, the miles slipped past under my feet, the concrete world of man was no more than a suggestion in my peripheral vision, but I was very aware of the roll of the natural landscape, hillocks and dips and valleys. We strolled down the hill that would have been Pond Street in the human world, the royal free hospital, no more than a bank of clouds on our right, into the valley where the ponds and springs fed the embryonic river fleet.

We continued due north out of Hampstead and arrived at 'The Barrow' on the heath. It did not look as I remembered it.

It was fully dark by now and *The Barrow* hunched against the skyline, crowned by its copse of trees. It was the huge double doors that were new, however. They definitely weren't there last time I came. They were ornate wooden doors with huge iron hinges, and the golden light of many candles flooded out of them over the grass.

I could hear the music of violins on the night air.

We approached the entrance and were greeted by a uniformed footman who took our names, or the names of my fellows at least, I'd obviously passed myself off as a servant rather too well. I waited close to the door inside what turned out to be a huge, candle lit hall, and Cass and Davi gave me their hats.

Dancers swirled to the violins and a long table groaned with food and drink of every kind. I made a mental note not to touch a morsel or drink a drop at any cost. All the folklore says that accepting refreshment from the little people is a sure-fire way to be trapped in their world, which is all well and good until you return home and find that a hundred years have elapsed.

I found myself cradling Cass and Davi's hats in one hand and gripping the little rowan knife with the other, so I consciously tried to relax and watched events unfold. The hall was wide and long and lit by many candle filled candelabras, casting a yellowish glow on the pikes and swords which lined the walls like trophies of a hundred wars. All of the guests were sumptuously dressed in rich colours and floaty silks, and the music was overlaid with their excited chatter. I reminded myself that traditionally much of the glamour of a fairy court was just glamour and nothing more. At dawn, the candles would revert to fireflies in the grass and the fine food and wines into berries and mushrooms, and the dew of the fields and woods.

The queue which my companions had joined wound through the throng, and at its end was a very overdressed person brandishing a pair of lorgnettes, through which he peered at each guest as they were presented and nodded patronisingly down his long nose at them. His outfit was truly spectacular, a waistcoat sewn with sequins, or perhaps diamonds, it was so sparkly in the candlelight. A long, silver-grey coat with frogging and a high collar, matching breeches, leaf green hose and very, very pointed patent shoes with silver buckles.

His bony head was topped by a powdered wig and adorned by a beaty spot on one cheek. He had something of the French aristo from the revolutionary era about him, I thought. As each guest approached a herald announced them to the gathering.

"Mistress Catalina Honeybrow of Maresbury," he recited, "Royal seamstress by appointment." The duke kissed her hand and smarmed something to her, then repeated the exercise with Meg, or 'Mistress Megan De Prix of Maresbury' as I now knew her to be. Cassivellaunus was next up.

"Master Cassivellaunus of that ilk, bespoke carpenter, joiner and cabinet maker of this kingdom," recited the herald, and then Davi, "Master Davidillidallion Hollyfoot, bespoke carpenter, joiner and cabinet maker."

Presentations over, my colleagues melted into the crowd, and I was left at the threshold clutching their hats. Thankfully, no one took any notice whatsoever of a flunky at the door. I caught a glimpse of Davi at the buffet, unsurprisingly, and

Catalina and Meg lined up opposite the gentlemen for the next gavotte, or whatever these ritualised dances were. Waiters scurried between the guests carrying silver platters laden with delicacies, and His Grace, I noticed, was constantly surrounded by a throng of sycophantic admirers, agreeing heartily with everything he said. He was less polished in his dealings with his staff, however.

He cuffed one server around the back of the head for some slip or oversight, and the servant backed away from him, bowing as low as he could, all the way out of the hall. All his people seemed seriously afraid of him, and I began to decide that I didn't like His Grace at all. I could quite see why Cass and Davi didn't want or need him as a customer, and whilst I was waiting, I began thinking about how to uncouple them from his patronage.

The evening dragged on in a whirl of candle lit dances, until Cass and Davi appeared out of the throng, well fed and overheated in their formal coats.

"We've said our 'thankyous', so I think we can politely get out of here now" said Davi, "The girls won't be coming just yet, they're busy." I could see Catalina dancing with a distinguished looking gentleman in a splendid green topcoat, so I handed

Cass and Davi their hats and we headed out into the clear night air.

I'd began to worry about the glamour wearing off before I got home. I had my Oyster card with me so I could get on the tube at Belsize park, but I'd be wearing a wing collar and tabs, and better still I'd be carrying an illegal fixed blade knife.

I began rehearsing my excuses for the British Transport Police; "I know it *is* an offensive weapon officer, but it's made of Rowan and iron and I'm carrying it purely as a talisman against the evil workings of the fae—" I didn't think that would wash.

The glamour which Catalina had put on me was holding out, however, which was just as well as she was still fully occupied at the Ducal ball.

The walk back was equally as weird as the walk there had been. Again, manmade features receded into the background, and natural ones were vivid and imposing. I'd never realised that I lived on top of a hill before! I began to wonder just how long I'd remain a foot tall. That would be a tough one to explain away to Lorraine and Linda — "There *are* fairies at the bottom of the garden after all, and they shrank me—"

We arrived very quickly at the summer house and sat on the veranda considering the evening's events.

"The girls enjoy these evenings I know," said Cass, "but personally I hate them. And to be honest I hate His Grace, too." I nodded agreement to this.

"I saw the way he treats his staff," I said. "I certainly wouldn't work for him."

Cass looked pityingly at me and explained, "they're bonded slaves, they don't have any choice in the matter, they just have to keep their heads down and hope that they don't end up executed, or worse, for some imagined offence." I wondered what could be worse than execution, but decided it wasn't the time to ask.

"All right," I said, "so we definitely need a plan to get you two out from under his patronage. I understand that you can't just tell him that you don't want his business, but what if *he* dropped *you?*" They considered this for a moment, but there were problems.

"He knows we're the best," explained Cass. "Do you remember that cabinet we made for his war trophies, Davidillidallion? It had a glass panelled section for weapons and armour, drawers for medals, spikes for heads, everything."

Davi nodded. "Oh yes, we've made some nice pieces for him over the years." I persevered. "Would the fact that you're working for a human put him off?" I asked. "There must be issues with prejudice and snobbery around the fact that, well, let's not pull punches, I'm paying you to make children's toys." They considered this.

"It certainly would," Cass declared, "but I for one don't fancy going to the Ducal Palace, seeking an audience and stating that I'd rather work for a man than the duke. It would be a pretty good way of guaranteeing that you came home as a toad or some such."

"I see that," I said, "but what if it somehow got back to him, without involving you two at all? If a rival, someone like Pandemonious Balker for instance, found out that you two were working for me, would he want the duke to know?"

"He sure as Hades would!" exclaimed Davidillidallion. "He'd be straight over to the Heath seeking an audience and offering his own nasty handiwork. And good luck to him!"

"But," said Cassivellaunus, "who would tell Balker? He wouldn't believe the girls, he knows we work pretty closely with them and he'd suspect something. I wouldn't trust Thorfinn or Martin to get it right, to be perfectly honest, no offence, and who else is there?"

I said, "I'll do it," then thought 'you must be totally insane'. They considered this.

"Hmm. If we got Catalina to put the glamour on you again, we could take you to Balker's 'factory' as he likes to call it, and you could walk right into his 'so called' office and scare him to death. Brilliant! How would you tell him though?"

"Well," I said, "I'd probably say that you two had a commission to make doll's house furniture for me, but that some Duke or other was making demands on your time, and because he's so exalted and you were so anxious to please him, my work was getting held up, and I wasn't very satisfied. I'd ask if he could take it on instead because I'd heard he had a modern, efficient manufacturing business."

Slow smiles were spreading across their little weathered faces.

"Oh yes, he'd like that, but he'd be mortified that a man could see him at all, never mind that you'd heard of his business. He'll instantly see that you're a man, even though you'll be a proper person's height."

"Good," I said. "I'll scare him half to death, emphasise that you're both totally committed to pleasing the duke but that I think you're an old-fashioned business that can't cope with demand, and ask him to take on my project, which of course he'll refuse. He'll then run straight to the duke and pass that on, which should get you sacked but not executed. If Balker gets the duke's work all the better. It sounds like he deserves it."

We drank a cup of *Cat's Eye* to that; it was a sound deal. I realised I was holding the little wooden cup between finger and thumb, and that I'd returned to my proper size, so I said goodnight to Cassivellaunus and Davidillidallion and headed indoors to tell Linda and Lorraine how boring it had been down the garden in the dark.

"Told you it was all nonsense," they'd say.

His Grace the Grand Duke

9. Business scam

Catalina couldn't find time to visit Cass and Davi for a couple of days. She and Meg had apparently picked up a couple of commissions during their evening at the Ducal Ball and needed to travel to the wharf on the river Brent to collect a consignment of organza from France so as to get started on them.

"How do you get a consignment of fabric from France to a wharf on the Brent, for heaven's sake?" I asked.

Davi gave me one of his pitying looks and explained that, obviously, you loaded it onto a ship in France, sailed it across the channel, up the Thames to Brentford, then up the Brent to our neck of the woods. Anyway, it seemed she could come over today at around noon, so I said I'd be at the summer house then, and we'd take it from there.

I duly turned up at ten to twelve to find Cass and Davi, Catalina and Meg chatting on the veranda. Catalina turned her attention to me and considered me with a long, cool stare.

"This one's virtually able to see us unaided," she purred. "I think you two have habituated it. There's something a little bit fae about it, too. Some of them are you know."

I had knelt down to be able to talk to them civilly, and now she turned my head to one side then the other with her long cool fingers on my cheek, the better to study me. It dawned on me that she was assessing me much like a potential buyer eyes up a horse.

She finally deemed it fit to address me directly and said, "I'll put the glamour on you as I did before, man, and you'll be able to walk into Balker's workshop and address him directly." She reached up and laid her fingertips on my forehead, then recited the same formula as before, and again I experienced that weird shift of focus, as the manmade faded to insignificance and the natural world was highlighted. Now standing one foot tall, I was ready to begin our bid to free Cass and Davi from the yoke of His Grace's patronage.

The three of us made our way through the gardens of the neighbourhood, ducking through holes in fences and keeping to the cover of bushes and flower borders, which I can assure you feels quite normal when you are a foot tall. We arrived at a garden with a large modern workshop, which I couldn't place in the human world at all. Time and space seemed so distorted under the influence of the glamour that I really couldn't say how far we'd travelled, although I knew we'd travelled South because we'd kept the morning sun to our left.

At the back of the manmade workshop was a sliding metal door, the same size as Cass and Davi's door but otherwise bearing no relation to it. There was a keypad next to it, but Cassivellaunus whispered that the door was unlocked during 'office hours', which were what Balker kept, apparently. We eyed up our target from the cover of a holly bush.

"His office is straight ahead at the back of his so-called factory," said Cass, with sincere contempt. "You can walk straight in and hopefully catch him in there. He has a couple of 'employees', but I think they'll be too amazed to do anything. You're pretty clearly a man, you know, despite your height, so ham it up, scare the willies out of him, then just turn tail and walk out, and meet us back here."

I remembered the 'rule of five' which my son had taught me. When you're *really* reluctant to do something, count to five, and on five just do it anyway. It does work. Try it sometime. I took a deep breath, counted one, two, three, four, five, walked up to the door and slid it wide open. Two characters were leaning over a bench as I strode in, but they jerked upright as they took in what had just walked through the door.

"Morning gents," I said breezily, and marched straight through to the glass walled office at the back. It reminded me forcefully of my very first job in a county court. We all worked in a large open plan office and the office manager sat in his glass walled office where he could keep an eye on us. Pandemonious Balker had an orderly office with rows of labelled files on a shelf and a safe in the corner, and he was sitting at a dark, polished desk behind a huge double columned ledger, staring unbelievingly at me through his round, steel rimmed spectacles. He was a tubby little individual, his belly swelling his dark waistcoat and presenting its brass buttons to the world. His beard was tidy and trimmed, unlike those of my good friends, and rather than the generic stripey hat with a tassel, he wore a round smoking cap in dark red velvet. I pulled myself up to my full twelve inches and smiled broadly at him.

"Good morning, Master Balker," I said in my deepest and most manly voice. "Or shall I call you Pandemonious? You don't mind if I call you Pandemonious, do you?"

"What, who, how?" he spluttered. He stood up, realised he was trapped behind the gigantic desk and sat down again. "How did you get in here, man?" he managed eventually.

"Why, through the front door, Pandy," I replied brightly. "I hope I didn't startle your employees too much." He swivelled his eyes around and dabbed his brow with a large spotted handkerchief. He looked like he was about to yell for the said employees, so I took advantage of the element of surprise and leaned across the desk at him, planting my hands on his ledger disrespectfully. "I've come to engage your services," I said, in the most imperious voice I could manage. "I've been employing two carpenters called, Cassivellaunus and Davidillidallion Hollyfoot, but to be honest I've been disappointed. They haven't finished my commission on time because of other work they're doing for a Grand Duke, or someone. It seems as though he takes priority over me, to the extent that they only really care about getting his furniture finished. I heard that your company is up to date, efficient and highly reliable, so I'm offering to switch my contract to you. I've come for a quote, Pandy."

He sat back like a deflated beach ball and stared at me, "I cannot under any circumstances take work from a man," he said. "It would be unethical and wrong, and it would damage my reputation among the folk. I must ask you, please, to leave my premises."

I straightened up. "Are you quite sure?" I asked, "I could reward you handsomely."

He hesitated at this, but then shook his head vigorously and said, "No, no, no, out of the question, quite out of the question."

"Very well, good day to you," I said, and turning on my heel strode straight out of the door, scattering the two carpenters who had crept closer to listen. I felt a strong urge to run at top speed into the holly bush, but just about managed a measured stride into the shrubbery, and back to an expectant Cass and Davi.

"Well, how did it go," asked Cassivellaunus.

But I said, "Can we get out of this neighbourhood first? It was a bit tense, and I'd be happier to get home then talk it over."

It was surprising what a difference scale made, and right now I didn't feel too comfortable around Balker's workshop and his staff.

"Let's go," said Cass, and we threaded our way through the shrubbery and under the fence, probably even more furtively than we'd come. Back on familiar turf we sat side by side on the summer house veranda and I told my tale.

"There were two carpenters in the factory, but I think they were too gobsmacked to move when I marched through the door, so I went straight to Balker's office and caught him at his desk with his nose in a ledger."

"Sounds about right," nodded Cass, "I don't think he spends much time with a tool in his hand these days."

"Anyhow," I said, "he was pretty amazed to see me at all, and a bit scared I think, so I took advantage and straight away offered him my contract, I stressed that you two were keen to fulfil His Grace's every desire for furniture, at the expense of my job, and that I was fed up. I did ham it up a bit and emphasise that I'd heard all about his brilliant modern methods, so hopefully he'll be living in terror of a queue of humans forming outside his factory!"

"Excellent," exclaimed Cass, "it sounds like you did everything you could. Now we wait to see if it works and Balker goes running off to tell His Grace."

"Well, I hope so," I said. "I left him reeling and walked straight out, so I expect he'll be thinking it through, but he knows you've been working for a human, and he'll see a business opportunity, I think."

At about this point I noticed the tingling which accompanied a return to full human stature, and the world filtered back to normality. It was interesting to think how my urge to get away from Pandemonious and his henchmen had evaporated, now that I was several dozen sizes bigger than him.

Size does matter in nature, I thought, but don't underestimate the little guy, you never know what qualities he might be hiding.

Pandemonious Balker

We went about our normal business after that, which for me entailed assisting the girls in their mammoth house clearance operation. They had already worked through all the storage boxes from the loft which contained old schoolbooks, their mum and dad's mementos, work certificates and awards, the complete official Cliff Richard calendars back to 1987, and everything else which you can't bring yourself to throw away but will in all likelihood never look at again.

They had reduced them from twenty-two to eleven boxes. My only commitment was to physically move them to the lounge and then back again. Good lockdown exercise.

After a couple of days, I noticed that a little green flag was flying from the summer house porch. This was the agreed sign that Cass and Davi wanted to see me, and it was suitably innocent for me to pass off as one of my many eccentricities. I headed down the garden to see what the deal was, and they were waiting for me with broad grins on their little faces.

"Excellent news," began Cassivellaunus, "it worked perfectly. We got a letter by crow this morning — look!" I spread out the little parchment sheet and read:

"From His Grace the Grand Duke Ignaceous De Beremond of Fleet

To Masters Cassivellaunus and Davidillidallion Hollyfoot, carpenters and joiners. Let it be known that His Grace has dispensed with the services of the above-mentioned tradesfolk with immediate effect. Their labours will no longer be required, and they are jointly and severally commanded by His Grace to refrain and desist from any further attendance at the Ducal Palace or at any of the establishments within the domains of His Grace. Failure to so comply will result in their apprehension and execution with the greatest prejudice in the form of a public spectacle. So is it writ and recorded in the Ducal record of the Dukedom of Fleet.

This 57th day of the year of the inverted Oak in the era of the Great Warming.

By my hand

Grand Duke Ignaceous De Beremond."

"But this looks a lot like you've been banished on pain of execution?" I said, "are you sure it's good news?"

"It's excellent news!" replied Davidillidallion, "if you read between the lines, it means that we'll never have to attend one of those gods forsaken Ducal balls any more, and we don't get stuck with making himself a lot of random furniture for no payment. I for one will be delighted never to go near the Ducal estates again."

"Hear, hear," said Cassivellaunus. "Ditto." All seemed to be well after all then, despite the tone of the Ducal letter.

"He always gets them to write like that, it's his style," explained Davi.

"Another good reason not to work for him them, then" I said.

We drank a cup of *Old Cats Eye* to celebrate the good news, and Cassivellaunus and Davidillidallion said they'd now turn their attention to my doll's house furniture on a full-time basis. All was well with the world, or so it would seem.

10. Gone West

As Spring progressed so did work on the doll's house furniture. An excellent little set of kitchen units appeared, although admittedly the cooker looked more of an Aga and less of a state of the art fan assisted model. It was followed by a dining table and four chairs and a really nice little set of shelves that would fit in a corner. Lockdown restrictions were still a problem, but I carefully boxed the items up with lots of packing and posted them to North Weald. Lorraine's friend was over the moon and sent messages with a video of her granddaughter playing with the furniture in the restored doll's house. I took my 'phone down the garden and showed this to Cassivellaunus and Davidillidallion, who I think were really impressed that their work could provide such deeply absorbing pleasure, although of course neither of them would say so.

In due course the kitchen furniture was followed by a sofa and armchair, gorgeously upholstered in a gold and brown stripe, complete with matching cushions. I detected the hand of

Mistress Catalina and Meg here. There was also a bookcase and a coffee table in matching and rather beautiful pale ash. I created a dozen tiny books myself, with coloured card covers and real pages. I gave them titles like 'Little Women', 'Little House on the Prairie' and 'The Doll's House'. Again, I packed the whole lot in a cardboard box with masses of tissue paper and cotton wool and got them in the post to North Weald.

Then all activity ceased. No more furniture, no green flag flying on the summer house, no barely audible whistling and hammering. I went down the garden to knock on the green door and found it unlocked, so I tapped on it anyway and looked inside. There was nothing beyond it except the blind cedar planks of the summer house itself. No little room, no other dimensional workshop, no magic.

I had to sit down at the patio table. I was so accustomed to finding Cassivellaunus and Davidillidallion at work at the bottom of the garden that their total absence was a real shock. There wasn't really much I could do, I decided, other than wait. I had no means of contacting any of the other 'Little Folk' I had been privileged enough to meet, and no idea where Cass and Davi might be if not in the garden. Each morning I'd go out to exercise, but my first stop was always at the summer house, to check for a presence. There never was one.

The little green door had disappeared and there was no sign that it had ever been there. After a week of this I stopped checking, it was pointless and obsessional anyway. After a couple of weeks, I decided that my relationship with the world of the fae might well have ended, and that I'd just have to get on with human life in the human world, like everybody else.

Spring transitioned into Summer and the three of us spent much more time outdoors, gardening, reading in the sunshine and fitting in a barbeque whenever it was warm enough. I have to admit that the barbeques still gave me a pang. I'd catch myself thinking 'the lads will be watching, I'll save them a sausage', then kick myself under the patio table for being sentimental. I had pretty much adjusted to life without tiny carpenters though, I'd taken back ownership of my own garden, and even next door's tabby had ventured out into the sun and seemed to be recovered, although I noticed that she gave the birch tree a wide berth.

Towards the end of summer, I was sitting outside at dusk, watching the bats, when a greenish phosphorescence at the bottom of the garden caught my eye. I'd long ago given up looking for signs of Cass and Davi, but there was something most odd down there, so I ambled down the path to take a look. On the veranda of the summer house was a little silky envelope about three inches square. It was a pale colour, and glowed with an inner light of its own, which is why I'd noticed it. Embroidered on the front in an elegant hand was my name, 'Geoffrey Christopher Denman Esq'.

Gingerly but with increasing excitement I picked it up, opened the flap and took out the sheet of delicate paper it contained. A simple message was written in the same genteel hand responsible for the embroidery:

'Mr Geoffrey,
attend at Maresbury Dell at dusk on the night of the full moon.
I have intelligence which you will wish to learn.
Felicitations and kind regards.
Mistress Catalina Honeybrow of Maresbury'.

The Dell was a little local park, a pocket park embedded in the streets of the neighbourhood. Volunteers maintained it and it was a magical little site, even without the presence of Mistress Catalina. The full moon was in two nights time, I learned online, so I made my excuses around the theme of an after dark bat-watch-walk and waited impatiently.

At the appointed time I headed over to the Dell and sat on a bench by the fish pond, just as the last of the sunset faded and night crept in. The little park was unlit and soon became very dark, so that I was peering into the gloom with dilated pupils when a smooth female voice at my left shoulder nearly gave me a heart attack. Mistress Catalina had arrived with total stealth and was standing on the bench next to me, resplendent in a ground length bottle green gown with a frilly silver cape over her shoulders.

"Good evening, Mr Geoff," she intoned. "I see that you are well. I bring news of your friends of this kingdom, Cassivellaunus and Davidillidallion."

I couldn't really believe my ears; I suppose if I'm honest I have to admit that I was starting to wonder if I'd imagined the whole fairy furniture episode. "Thank you so much, Mistress Catalina," I managed. "Yes please, do tell me, I've been worried about them, and really puzzled about what happened."

She smiled indulgently and took her time sitting down next to me and arranging her gown just so. When she was quite satisfied, she continued. "Your ruse to disentangle them from their dealings with the grand duke worked very well, and I think they were both delighted with the outcome. None of us, though, had taken account of what a poisonous weasel Master Pandemonious Balker is, although with hindsight perhaps we should have realised."

"I did put the frighteners on him though," I said, "and I didn't think he'd be a problem, to be honest. Plus, presumably, he got the duke's contract for furniture."

She nodded and said "He was indeed terrified, but once he realised that his position in His Grace's favour was secure, he evidently began plotting his revenge. Fairly or not, he blamed his fright on our mutual friends, and did everything in his power to blacken their names and reputations."

That gave me pause for thought. The last thing I would have intended was that any harm should come to Cass or Davi.

Mistress Catalina continued. "Once the weasel was installed as His Grace's official cabinet maker, he offered his services to all the folk at reduced rates, undermining Cassivellaunus and Davidillidallion, who he described as being fit only to make crude toys for the offspring of men. He also called them traitors to the folk and accused them of revealing sacred rites and secrets to your kind. Sadly, a number of folk I knew took advantage of his offers, and our friends were marginalised in their trade so that some suppliers wouldn't deal with them. I think his poisonous words also had their effect, because they received some very threatening letters and had to ward off one or two seriously vicious curses."

I shook my head sadly. "Oh, dear God, I'd never intended that," I said. "It all seemed to work out so well."

"Don't distress yourself," Catalina responded, "It was purely the venom of Master Balker which was responsible for the eventual downfall of our friends." I didn't like the sound of this at all, and prompted her to get on with it, but the lady had obviously rehearsed her account and continued at her leisure. "Once he had the ear of the Grand Duke, Pandemonious Balker created a complete fiction in an attempt to damage our friends. He falsely accused them of neglecting His Grace's commissions to make furniture for men, and of stealing His Grace's precious veneers and gold leaf to attract human customers. The fatal fiction which he invented however was that they were planning the demise of the Dukedom. Balker convinced His Grace that Cassivellaunus and Davidillidallion were in league with human plotters who would excavate the ducal palace to build something called a 'skate park' and banish His Grace from the kingdom."

This sounded a bit thin, but then I knew next to nothing about the psychology of the folk, and what sounded ludicrous to me might be enough to get Cass and Davi executed.

Catalina continued. "His Grace has ultimate authority within the Dukedom, and commonly executes those who offend him, simply on a whim. After the execrable rodent Balker had poisoned his mind, His Grace ordered that Cassivellaunus and Davidillidallion should be arrested forthwith and brought before him at the Ducal Palace for sentencing."

"But hold on a minute," I said, "I understood they were banned from the palace on pain of death?"

"Precisely," she replied. "The sentence would have determined what form those deaths should take."

I sat in a bit of a proverbial stunned silence after this. What had seemed like a prank, almost a practical joke, had turned out to be life threatening.

Mistress Catalina composed herself then continued. "Do not fear. Masters Cassivellaunus and Davidillidallion understood the seriousness of their situation and knew that time was short. They gathered the essentials they would need and left this kingdom immediately. Long ago now they took ship and have gone into the West."

I gave this some thought before I responded. I knew that traditionally there were fairy kingdoms unknown to men which were invariably in 'The West', but I suspected that I'd never find out from Catalina whether the lads were in the mythical realm of Tir Na Nog, or just lying low somewhere in County Kerry.

"So, can they be contacted?" I asked.

She shook her head slowly and stared me down. "No, Mr Geoff, even I do not know their precise whereabouts. All is not lost though. I have certain, connections, shall we say, and I am working with well-connected and influential friends to rehabilitate Cassivelaunus and Davidillidallion. Do not give up hope, Mr Geoffrey, the folk are long, long lived and very resilient. I shall contact you again when I have further intelligence." With that she wasn't there any more. She didn't leave or disappear or anything, she just ceased to be there.

My tryst with Mistress Catalina had really given me food for thought. A few days ago, I had, to be honest, pretty much put my dealings with the folk behind me. Now I was catapulted back into those manic early days when I'd been shrunk to attend a fairy ball and rescued a tiny carpenter from next door's cat. I found myself sitting outside until late, squinting into the gloom to see if there was a tell-tale firefly glow down at the summer house.

It was whilst sitting outside pretending to study bats that a thought occurred to me. I went inside to fetch one of my old diaries, because I'd remembered that I'd recorded all the characters of the Elder Futhark, the old Norse Runic alphabet, in it. I'd become a bit rusty now and probably didn't know my Ansuz from my Algiz any more, but it came back to me after studying my notes for a while.

The next day I headed out to the garden with a sharp knife and cut some ash. Yggdrasil, the World Tree of Norse mythology, has always been said to be ash, although I know there's now a pretty good case for it to have been yew. Anyhow, I've always liked ash, so I used it to cut plenty of slim, three-inch sticks and skinned the bark so that they glowed white. I left them to dry out on the workshop bench and went inside to ask the girls if they fancied chilli for dinner.

The following day, equipped with my sticks and my surplus chilli, I planned to head down the garden and set a runic message for any passing crows to read [or an invitation to lunch, whichever the case may be]. I had considered what sort of language might catch a crow's attention and appeal to it strongly. I settled on.

'Food here,
Come down,
Message to carry'.

I hoped that wasn't patronising. I could imagine two crows schmoozing on a branch.

"Do you know, darling, it addressed me like a tiny chick."

"How very degrading, my dear."

Anyhow, I carefully wrote the message in the tiniest hand I could manage, using Chinese black ink which is waterproof. I wrote on thin card, which was lightweight but strong, and hoped that it didn't get waterlogged and disintegrate. After all it had to get at least as far as county Kerry, and possibly much further. The message took some thought as it could only be a very few words, but in the end, I settled on saying.

'So sorry it went bad.
So unexpected.
Have worried, let me know plans.
Hope you are well.
Best
G'

The next hurdle was the small matter of attaching it to the crow's leg. I stepped back from the exercise at this point and thought, "it's happening again. They've got me considering how to employ a crow, and they're not even here!"

Anyhow, after considering an elastic band and various other fixings, I decided to use some light cotton thread which would hold the message securely but would snap if the bird somehow got it entangled in twigs or whatever.

Finally prepared, it was time to put the plan into action. I headed to an open patch of lawn and started setting out my runes. I'd waited until Linda and Lorraine were out because I didn't really want to have to explain the endeavour. I had divided the chilli into two little takeaway containers, one for an immediate reward and one held in reserve until after the message was attached. *If* the message was attached.

Promisingly, a large glossy black crow soon alighted on the opposite side of the lawn and tilted his head from one side to the other, no doubt considering whether chilli was worth getting close to a human for. I knelt on the grass so as to seem less enormous, and proffered one of the treats, keeping the other visible but out of reach. The corvid approached cautiously but edged close enough to quickly devour the first portion of chilli, his bill clacking on the plastic pot. When he had finished gulping, he eyed me beadily and looked pointedly at the second helping. I slowly held up the little card cylinder and opened my other hand, suggesting that the bird came closer, I hoped. He eyed the remaining chilli some more, then hopped close enough for me to touch him. Here goes nothing, I thought, and slowly extended the card tube, using my other hand to gently loop the thread around his scaly black leg. I tied a good knot and resisted breathing a loud sigh of relief, then handed over the rest of the bribe. Now came the tricky bit because I didn't have any precise delivery instructions for my courier.

"Cassivellaunus and Davidillidallion Hollyfoot," I said slowly. "In the far west." That was the best I had.

The crow blinked, cawed three times (which is pretty deafening up close, I can tell you) and clawed himself into the air, turning and flapping off pretty much due west, which was encouraging. I watched him dwindle into the London haze, then headed inside to await developments.

No events developed. After a week I gave up waiting and decided that I'd wasted my chilli and burdened an innocent but unhelpful bird with a tube of card for a few days, although knowing how clever crows are, he had no doubt removed it within a few minutes. I pictured him back on the branch chatting with his mate again:

"They hand over meaty treats pretty freely, but they like to tie one of these on your leg. No problem though — look — you can just peck it off. Easy. See?"

I felt that I'd be giving up a bit easily if I didn't make one more attempt, so on a sunny day I fetched my remaining ash twigs and another two helpings of a meaty treat and headed down the garden. Again, I wrote the same runes then sat back and waited. There wasn't a lot of bird activity today, but after a while a crow flapped by, circled to look closer, then came in for landing. I slowly moved out onto the lawn, offered the first food package, and waited, keeping as still as I could manage. I could have sworn it was the same bird, but then they do look very similar to me.

In any case he soon hopped closer, cocked his head to assess me, then quickly gobbled the treat. *Clack, clack, clack.* I had started moving my hands nearer and was now allowed to loop the thread around one leg and lightly tie it on. I proffered the second offering and waited, immobile. When he was all done and had wiped his impressive bill on the grass, he fixed me with those beady black eyes just as though he was awaiting instructions. There is a definite steely intelligence in the eyes of crows, quite different to human intelligence, but quite real. They can, after all, distinguish numbers up to thirty.

I had a feeling this one would know if he was owed thirty lunches and only got twenty nine. I had considered the delivery instructions more carefully this time and said clearly. "Cassivellaunus and Davidillidallion Hollyfoot, in Tir Na Nog."

He blinked and stared, stared and blinked at this. I knew that the traditional way to get to the mythical 'Land of Promise' was by travelling to westernmost Ireland, then continuing westward on the path made by the setting sun across the Atlantic. I couldn't see my courier doing that for a crop full of chilli somehow. Nevertheless, he bowed and cawed three times then flapped into the air, turning westward and heading off over the gardens and rooftops.

I hadn't realised Lorraine had been watching this episode. Now she startled me by saying, "Very impressive! Did you train it to do that, or do you think you just have a rapport with crows?"

"Well," I responded, standing and rubbing my hands clean, "they are about the most intelligent birds, scientists reckon they're up there with a seven-year-old human, you know. They've done tests and found they can tell one human from another, use tools and have reasoning abilities. Think of the old Aesop's fable about the crow displacing water with stones to get to the treat!"

"Hmm," she said. "That one can certainly spot a sucker with a bowl of chilli! I don't know what you're like, really, but at least you're harmless I suppose. Lucky, I love you!" Phew. I was relieved not to be explaining that in any more detail.

I looked up the daily range of a crow which turned out to be forty or fifty miles. The farthest point west in Kerry was nearly 600 miles, meaning that, theoretically, it could take twelve days there, a rest period, and twelve days back. Call it a month to build in leeway, then.

Distractions offered by meaty treats were probably a factor here. How long it would take to reach Tir Na Nog and come back was truly anyone's guess, but in any case, I was determined to put it out of my mind for the next month.

I did this quite successfully actually, there was plenty to do in the garden and around the house, and there were always carving and painting ideas to try out, so that when there was a persistent cawing outside one afternoon, I took no notice at all, until Lorraine said, "that damned crow's very persistent, he's not one of your experimental victims is he?"

The penny dropped and I got outside as quickly as I could without arousing suspicion. It was indeed my courier crow, perched in the pear tree and shouting for attention as loudly as he could, which was pretty loudly. When I appeared, he glided down to the lawn and waddled towards me quite confidently. He'd obviously decided I was no threat, and an easy touch for a late lunch, to boot. Around one leg he carried a little tube, *not* my cardboard message. I calmed myself so as not to scare him and extended my hands slowly. He let me detach the tube quite patiently, but I suppose that if he'd flown here from county Kerry carrying it he was pretty relieved to be shot of it. Of course, once he was freed from his burden, he was immediately looking for a reward, which I didn't have on me. Feeling like a louse, I slipped the tube into my pocket and went straight to the fridge where a Tupperware box of cooked sausages presented themselves. Perfect. Taking one I headed back to my corvine colleague, who was waiting impatiently on the lawn, and offered him chunks of it, one at a time, until he'd devoured the lot, and I held up my empty hands in the universal sign for 'all gone'. The crow bobbed and cawed, then took to the air and headed off to the nearby ash trees where he perched and preened himself. It looked like this particular contract was over, then.

For my part I got inside my workshop as quickly as I could and popped the top off of the little tube. Inside was a tightly scrolled sheet which I unrolled and weighted at the ends to keep it from rolling up again. I read the message it contained:

'Mr Geoff,

Greetings from your exiled friends in the far west. We were both astonished to receive your message, your powers know no bounds! Please do not be concerned for us. This is a land of great hospitality, with music and dance, food and drink aplenty. We are still in hiding here, but our mutual friend [the one given to needlecraft] is working on our behalf at the royal court of our kingdom. She has connections with our royalty going back a very long time, longer than you might imagine, and is a blood relative, although she has great humility. We are hopeful that soon we shall be able to return to our old workshop and pick up our trade as it used to be, before all the recent unpleasantness. We have a grudge to settle also, and honour must be served. Do not fear for us but wait in good hope.

Our warmest regards

C and D H.'

I paused then read it again, mildly astonished by the fact that a garden crow had managed to exchange messages between London and who knows where, with almost no information to fly by. It was definitely from Cass and Davi, although where they were was still a mystery. The hospitable land of music and fine victuals could as easily be Kerry as Tir Na Nog. Somehow it was no surprise that Catalina had royal connections, although I did think it was stretching it a bit to credit her with humility. In any event there was little choice but to await developments.

As the crow flies

11. Developments

I impatiently got on with the daily routine, restraining myself from checking for waiting crows, or little green flags on the summer house. Days extended into weeks and then a month as Autumn loomed. It seemed that Mistress Catalina's efforts at court were taking an awfully long time to bear any fruit. The hot dry summer began to draw to an end, but it was still warm long into the evening, and the three of us often sat outside with a glass of cold white wine as dusk came and the bats ventured out around the crown of the giant plane tree at the end of the garden.

It is a magical time, the transition between day and night, light and dark, and perhaps between the dominance of mankind and that of other folk. As I gazed down the garden, I suddenly noticed a faint yellowish glow on the summer house veranda. Could it possibly be another missive from Mistress Catalina? I resisted jumping up immediately and had to wait until we jointly decided there was a risk of mosquitos, and it was time to move inside.

"I'll check we're all locked up out here," I said, and sauntered as casually as I could down the garden path. Sure enough there was another pale green envelope with my name on it, which I quickly slipped into my pocket before making a show of checking that the door was locked. At the first opportunity I sidled off to rip open my letter and devour the contents.

'Mr Geoffrey,

Greetings and felicitations to you and blessed be.

I have great good news which I would impart to you as soon as practicable. Meet with me at the old farmhouse on Dollis Hill at dusk on the night of the full moon, when I shall be able to explain the situation.

Best wishes

Mistress Catalina Honeybrow of Maresbury.'

Luckily, I thought I knew where the old farmhouse might be. In Gladstone Park stands the ruin of Dollis Hill House which had started life as a farm in the 19th century, but soon became a smart home in the country away from the buzz of London. Prime Minister Gladstone was often a guest there and used it as his refuge from Whitehall. He sometimes bathed in the little lake which is still there. Mark Twain stayed there too, he said it came nearer to being a paradise than any other home he ever occupied. Now only the floor plan remains, marked out in low walls like the ruins of a medieval castle. The full moon was, as before, in two nights time, so I made my plans (and my excuses) and waited.

Late in the evening on the appointed day I got myself over to Gladstone Park and headed up the hill towards the ruin. I made myself comfortable on the low wall of the old house, facing South, and watched the sun go down over Wembley in the west. Dollis Hill House is a very civilised ruin, it has a sign to tell you all about it and has been designated an 'outside performance space'. The floor plan is still very clear from the network of low walls. Just as before, Mistress Catalina was *not* there one moment and yet *was* there the next. She didn't seem to have come *from* anywhere. I was starting to believe there was a parallel dimension which her kind could move into and out of at will. She smiled sweetly at me and settled herself onto the wall at my side, arranging and smoothing her gown as she did so. This time it was a golden yellow shade with a fine embroidery of leaves and fruits.

"Blessed be, Mr Geoffrey," she began.

"And may you be blessed also, Mistress Catalina," I responded. "What news do you have? I've been dying of frustration waiting to find out what's become of Cass and Davi!"

She smiled to herself and said, "There are a great many things which men allow themselves to die of, in my experience, but allow me to tell you of all that has passed."

I took a deep breath and waited patiently while she rearranged her skirts, and finally continued. "As you know, Mr Geoffrey, Cassivellaunus and Davidillidallion Hollyfoot have been exiled in the west, and the weasel Balker has usurped their trade and their business here in the Brent valley. In the meantime, I have re-established contact with old friends at the royal court, and have sought an audience with the King, who you probably are not aware is His Royal Highness King Alberich XVI. His royal highness was magnanimous enough to hear my pleas, and only one moon since I attended an audience and explained all to him. Of course, I could not criticise our grand duke, but I am quite sure his royal highness knows the duke's character and must have heard of some of the tyrannies he has committed over the centuries. I did however explain that our friends are loyal subjects who have been treacherously undermined for crass commercial reasons. I am sure it was understood that the duke's, *tendencies*, shall we say, allowed two hard working and very skilled subjects to be exiled, and their business to fall into the hands of a scoundrel. I can be quite persuasive, you know, Mr Geoffrey."

I don't doubt it for a moment, I thought, but simply nodded and smiled.

Mistress Catalina resumed. "His royal highness heard me very graciously and said he would take counsel and decide what was to be done. I stayed with old friends, and whilst at court, incidentally, took some very profitable orders for fine couture. I must remember to place orders for golden silk and white satin so that they can be shipped in time. Anyway, in due course I received a royal communication from a herald, informing me that his highness intended to formally pardon Cassivellaunus and Davidillidallion, and license them to move and trade freely within the bounds of his realm. His highness has not implicated the grand duke in any way, which means that he can simply turn a blind eye to affairs, and our friends can avoid contact with him, which I am sure will please them greatly. His highness has not, however, addressed the injustice of the weasel's underhand dealings and the slur he has cast on our friends. That is also doubtless for political reasons, but I know it will leave Master Cassivellaunus filled with ire, and keen for vengeance. That, I predict, will be a problem we shall all have to face together."

I just sat for a while digesting this. It seemed the lads would be safely returning home, but under a cloud of unsettled business. I knew Cassivellaunus well enough to agree with Mistress Catalina. He would doubtless be fixated on revenge and on clearing his name. I could well imagine an ugly little vendetta breaking out at the bottom of the garden.

"Thank you very much, Mistress Catalina," I said eventually. "You have helped me understand the situation, I think. Cassivellaunus and Davidillidallion will return home quietly and without fuss, and the grand duke will totally ignore them, which is actually what they were hoping to achieve back in the spring. I agree, though, Cassivellaunus will have a serious grudge against weasel Balker, and will definitely want revenge. How far do you think he would go?"

She shook her head sadly and replied, "As far as putting Balker's head on a stick, I should imagine, Mr Geoffrey. Passions run high among the folk, and Master Cassivellaunus is of very old and very proud stock. I don't think anything can come between him and his revenge. In any event, let us prepare for their return, and hope that matters come out well. Farewell to you now, Mr Geoffrey." And with that she simply wasn't there.

I returned home and decided that there was no point in anticipating events. The most I could do was tidy up around the summer house, wait for the lads to arrive back from 'the west', and bake them a couple of loaves when they arrived.

12. Vendetta

Not a lot happened for a week or two. I had tidied up around the summer house and kept half an eye on it, but whether the lads were in County Kerry or Tir Na Nog, it seemed the return journey was taking some time. I had visions of them setting off on long travels in howdahs on the back of hedgehogs, then embarking on a tiny ship to cross the swelling Irish sea. I probably wasn't far off the mark.

Then one morning, when I set off to do my Ba Duan Jin on the bottom patio, there were signs of life. At long last! The little green door was back, in need of a coat of paint, and as I drew closer, I could hear cheerful whistling and vigorous sweeping from inside.

"Hello," I called, "anybody home?"

The sweeping stopped and Davidillidallion stuck his head out of the door. A broad smile spread across his little tanned face, and he stepped out, wiping his hands on his jerkin. He had a new jerkin, and indeed a whole new outfit, no doubt from 'out of the west'. It was mainly in the usual preferred shades of green and brown, but it was the stripey cap which caught the eye, a splendid new one in scarlet and white.

"Greetings, Mr Geoff!" He exclaimed. "My, it is good to see you, and to be back in your summer house again! I expect Mistress Catalina has told you about our adventures, but such a lot has happened to us in the far west since we went away. Come and sit on the veranda with me and I'll tell all." We sat in the pleasant Autumn sun and said nothing for a while, just enjoying each other's company again.

Eventually I asked, "How's Cassivellaunus? Is he all right?"

This seemed to cast a shadow for Davi, and he squirmed about a bit before replying. "He's not all right, not at all really, Mr Geoff," he said. "He took the whole affair very personally and he's sworn vengeance on Pandemonious Balker. He's glad to be back in the Brent valley, don't get me wrong, but he feels cheated out of his livelihood, and worse than that, he feels that his family name has been sullied. I don't think he'll get over it until honour is satisfied and all the folk acknowledge it."

Not good news, then. I'd hoped that time and travel might soften the injury, but evidently not.

"Is he here now, Davi? Can I talk to him?" I asked. Davi shook his head and his jaunty cap tassel swung left to right. "'Fraid not, Mr Geoff," he replied. "He said he needed to make some arrangements and that he'd be gone for a day or two. I've got a bad feeling he's hiring some paid fighters to stand at his back when he challenges Balker."

Oh dear. This didn't sound good at all. The grand duke would doubtless ignore the lads with a royal pardon backing them, but he couldn't very well ignore a turf war, with mercenaries, on his Ducal doorstep.

"Can't he be persuaded?" I ventured, "it sounds like he might blow your royal pardon if he starts up a private war in my back garden."

"I don't think he can," replied Davidillidallion sadly. "His family honour is the most important thing in his life, even if it means permanent banishment. It would be a shame to leave the valley of the Brent forever, but it might come down to that." I thought on that for a while. It seemed grossly unfair to Davi, so I felt I had to point this out.

"But do you agree?" I tried, tentatively. "I understand that Cass is very insulted and very angry, but you have a life here too. Do you feel the same?" He bridled at this and sat up very straight.

"I was apprenticed to Master Cassivellaunus some centuries ago now," he declared, "and he's the finest craftsman it's ever been my honour to work with. If he needs me, I'm in his shield wall, and my axe is his, no questions asked."

I looked at him a bit sadly but said, "I'm very impressed, Davi. That's real friendship, and you should be really proud of yourself." It seemed there wasn't much more to be said.

Cassivellaunus did appear the next day, and I went down to the summer house to greet him, to find him looking drawn and very serious. Revenge is clearly a taxing business.

"It's good to see you again, Master Cassivellaunus," I said, "You're looking well. I was so pleased to hear that you received a royal pardon and that you could come home to work in the valley of the Brent again."

"Good morning, Mr Geoff," he responded. His voice was a bit flat, and he wouldn't meet my eye. Something was definitely wrong. "I'm sorry if I'm a bit distracted," he continued, "I've been taking care of business, and it's been very tiring."

Then out of the workshop sauntered three really ugly characters. They were the same height as Cassivellaunus and Davidillidallion, but there the resemblance ended. They were well muscled and clearly very strong for their height, but it was their war gear which was striking. They wore boiled leather armour over their torsos, with metal plates at the shoulders and studs all over. Their various straps and harnesses supported long handled axes and ugly looking knives, and they wore tall boots with metal plates on the shins and hobnails in the soles. They had long plaited beards much like Cass and Davi, but their heads were shaven and decorated with swirling tattoos. Their leader, who I later found went by the name of, Guthrum Broadaxe, nodded and smirked at me, quite unbothered by the fact that I was human, and they swaggered off into the bamboo for some purpose probably too horrible to think about.

"They're, er, casual part time employees," explained Cass, weakly. "I'll need them for support, I'm going to challenge Pandemonious Balker and force him to apologise." More like challenge Pandemonious Balker and dice him into small cubes, I thought, but said nothing. I gave Cass enough rope, and he continued to hang himself. "I know it must look a bit bad, Mr Geoff, but it must be done. Balker stole our business and blackened our name, he blackened my name, and I can't let that pass. He has employees, four or five, and Davidillidallion and I can't confront him on our own, so I've hired in some professional help. That's all. Just business."

I sighed and knelt so as to be closer to his height. "I think we both know where this is going, Cassivellaunus," I began, "you'll challenge Balker, he'll protect his ill-gotten business interests and he'll order his unfortunate employees to back him up, and then your apes will really hurt someone, or kill someone. Or probably everyone, actually. The grand duke won't be able to ignore it, and you and Davidillidallion will be back on a ship into the west, if you're lucky. Except this time, you won't be coming back."

He hung his head, and nodded weakly, but said, "It can't be helped, Mr Geoff. It's a matter of honour." It seemed the die was cast.

I decided to try my best to deflect Cassivellaunus from his plan for vengeance. I started on Davidillidallion but without much success. He was intent on supporting his business partner whatever the outcome, and Cassivellaunus wasn't budging. Davi detested the fairy mercenaries, who had taken to lounging around on the veranda, interspersed with hunting small birds with crossbows in the shrubbery, but he wasn't open to discussing any change of plan. I asked him if he could contact Mistress Catalina for me, which he promised he would.

Mistress Catalina appeared in her usual disconcerting manner when I was sitting outside the following evening. There she was on the Patio table, under my nose, where before there had been only my book and my wine glass.

"Greetings to you, Mr Geoffrey," she intoned, and settled onto the spine of my book. "Master

Davidillidallion tells me that you have grave concerns for Master Cassivellaunus, but it is as I predicted when last we met. He will not swerve from revenge because it is a matter of honour, regardless of the consequences."

I leaned towards her and looked long and hard into her sparkly blue eyes. "Is there really nothing I can do to persuade them, Mistress Catalina?" I asked. "I count them both as friends, and it would be heart breaking if they were banished forever."

She shook her head sadly. "Honour matters more than life among the more traditional folk, Mr Geoff, although admittedly the weasel Balker is the exception which proves the rule. I really don't think you will be able to sway them from their course." And she was gone.

So, it really did seem that things were spiralling towards a bloodbath at the bottom of the garden. A suburban Ragnarok. Cassivellaunus' hired axes had taken to practicing on the bottom patio, hacking each other's round shields and wrestling across the flagstones. Thankfully, it seemed only I could see and hear them, although I rather wished I couldn't. It was like watching repeats of 'Spartacus' every evening. And then things seemed to come to a head. Davidillidallion was waiting for me on the veranda next morning, looking agitated.

He straight away blurted out, "It's tonight. Mr Geoff. We're going to fire Balker's workshop and deal with him and his workmen as they run out to avoid the flames." So, I thought, a hall burning. Very Viking. Very traditional.

"And are you going to take part in this hall burning, Davidillidallion?" I asked.

"Oh yes," he responded immediately. "Cassivellaunus needs me there, I'll be right beside him."

I had already considered my position on all this, and decided I wasn't going to be involved. I was convinced that Balker could be negotiated with and probably would make some form of retraction and apology, without any need for a hall burning and a massacre. Now I said so to Davi and told him I'd take no part in it.

He looked a bit crestfallen but said, "I know, Mr Geoff, and that's as it should be. This is a matter between the folk, and it must be settled between the folk. Think of us tonight though, Guthrum says we're going in at dusk."

Guthrum Broadaxe

Although I wasn't an active combatant, I did feel a sneaky regard for Cassivellaunus. He was leading his little army into a genuine little war, after all, so I dusted off my old birdwatching binoculars and positioned myself at a vantage point in the conservatory to watch him and his band head off. What I saw through my lenses was not what I had expected, however. Moving down the garden, keeping furtively to the flower bed and bushes, was a little force led by Pandemonious Balker. I adjusted my focus wheel and peered harder, but it was unmistakeably the weasel himself, with five of his employees from the factory, and three other thugs carrying the little folk equivalent of pickaxe handles (tack hammer handles, I suppose). I sat back and considered.

The weasel must have got wind of Cassivellaunus' plan and decided to make a pre-emptive strike. Certainly, Guthrum and his men had not exactly been discreet. They'd probably been swaggering around the whole neighbourhood boasting about what they'd do to Pandemonious. Now they looked close to being the victims of a hall burning themselves. Maybe not though. As I watched the green door of the workshop opened and Cass emerged, leading his little team. They marched across the veranda and onto the lawn before they realised that there was an opposing force trailing down the garden towards them. Both sides stopped in their tracks, and it was obvious that open conflict was now unavoidable. Guthrum's trio reacted first. Whatever else they might be they were certainly consummate fighters and formed up into a short shield wall with Cass and Davi in the middle. Pandemonious Balker with his bigger force of eight lined up opposite them.

I was just standing up and panicking about what I ought to do to prevent a bloodbath when all hell broke loose. From the hydrangea bush erupted next door's tabby in a veritable storm of stripey fur, teeth and claws. She went straight for the biggest, slowest target which of course was Pandemonious Balker, and pinned him to the grass by his coat tails. Everyone else scattered as fast as they could.

Very soon there was just the cat and her plaything on the lawn. Cats are incredibly cruel and quite merciless when they've got the measure of their victim, and now she let the weasel crawl away then hauled him back with her claws, repeatedly. Finally, she did that nightmare thing where they take the victim in their jaws, roll onto their back and kick it to death, and it was all over. Next door's tabby looked disappointed that the fun had ended, picked up what remained of Pandemonious Balker in her jaws and slipped off into the undergrowth with him, leaving his smoking cap and a couple of brass buttons on the grass.

I found myself praying that she didn't take the remains home and leave them on the hearth rug as a gift for her owner. I had visions of the place thronged with hordes of cryptozoologists in the morning. The whole episode had been a tense nightmare beyond description really, especially for Pandemonious, and I decided to wait until the morning before putting out feelers.

13. Calm after the storm

I allowed a couple of days for the dust to settle. I found that my senses had gradually changed so that I could now detect events in that other, parallel kingdom. I had become habituated, as Mistress Catalina had said. Keeping half eye on the bottom of the garden I noticed a glimpse of leather armour and tattooed scalps as something muscled through the bamboo and guessed that Guthrum Broadaxe and his squad had been paid off and had moved on to wreak havoc and inflict mayhem in other kingdoms. Davi would be delighted, at least. It was probably a good time to wander down the garden path and take stock of things.

At the summer house it seemed like business as usual. Work was being done in the workshop and I tapped on the door knocker to get attention. Cassivellaunus answered, which was surprising, and he seemed quite bright and cheerful.

"Good morning, Mr Geoff." He said, we'll come outside and sit with you a while and tell you all that passed."

With all three of us installed on the veranda, Cassivellaunus began his tale. Of course, I realised, they had no idea that I'd been watching events unfold, and in any case, they must have been fully bound up in those events. I kept my peace and nodded to signal that he should continue.

"Guthrum decided that we should burn Balker out of his factory, and deal with him and his people as they fled the flames," he began. "We were all tooled up and ready at dusk and set off to march over there as night fell. What we didn't know was that Balker already knew our plans, right down to the night and the timing. It seems Guthrum and his boys had been drinking and boasting at the market, shouting about what a mess they'd make of Balker, and I suppose he'd decided to get in first and turn the tables on us. It was the weirdest coincidence though," he continued, thoughtfully. "We headed out at precisely the same moment as Balker's force arrived here. Very odd. We faced off on your lawn, and I still think we'd have won! Balker had a bigger force, but Guthrum and his boys were professionals."

Davidillidallion looked up at this and commented dryly, "Guthrum and his boys were animals. Expensive ones too. I'm just delighted that they've moved on."

Cass nodded and said, "Paying them off was a problem. I pointed out that they hadn't actually fought anyone, and the only things they'd killed had been bluetits in the bushes."

"Scum," commented Davi.

"Anyway," continued Cass, "I offered them half pay and it all got very ugly. Guthrum reckoned they had a contract, and since Balker was dead and the contract was fulfilled, he demanded full payment in metal. In the end I paid him off to get rid of them."

"Scum," confirmed Davi. "Expensive scum."

"So, how did it end, on the lawn that night?" I prompted.

Cass looked me in the eye and replied, "To be totally honest, it was horrible, Mr Geoff. I hated Balker with a vengeance and I won't pretend otherwise, but I wouldn't have wished that on him." He fell silent and Davi took up the tale.

"The stalking death was at large that night, Mr Geoff. None of us knew that, but now, thinking about it, it was no surprise. Killing and death were on everyone's mind that night, so when the stalking death pounced out of the bushes, I suppose it was almost as though we had summonsed it. How strange that it went straight for Balker, though."

Not really, I thought, *he was twice as fat and twice as slow as the rest of you*, but I zipped my lip and Davi continued. "It was a horrible death for sure. But in the end, it was the God's will, and I'm glad neither of us struck the fatal blow."

I nodded as sagely as I could and said, "I think that's quite right, if I might say so. It was an act of God, no one killed him deliberately, but now honour has been satisfied, and you're both free to continue working here in the Brent valley. Plus, on the positive side, Balker launched the attack on you when he was killed. He was the aggressor, so no one could fairly hold you responsible." They both brightened up at this and agreed that was indeed the case.

Davidillidallion paused, and said a bit awkwardly, "There was one thing I've been wanting to ask you about, Mr Geoff. Something that's been on my mind for a while."

"Ask away, Davidillidallion," I replied.

He continued, "When we were in hiding in the west we received your message by crow. We thought you must have got help from Catalina or Meg, or from one of the folk at least. But the paper and the writing belonged to a man, not one of the folk. What I'm asking, I suppose, is how did you do it, Mr Geoff?"

I smiled at them and said, "I watched you cutting sticks and setting out runes on the grass to call the crow, and then rewarding him with chilli, so I thought I could cut my own runes easily enough. I learned the Elder Futhark years ago."

"You know the futhark?" he asked incredulously.

I nodded as wisely as I could and confirmed, "Oh yes, Davi. Many men know the futhark men invented it, after all."

He grinned at that and said, "I think you'll find Odin All Father discovered it and gifted it to man, actually, though I'm still mightily impressed. But that doesn't answer how you told the crow to deliver it, or how you knew where we were. How did that work? Did you get help from the folk for that?"

I shook my head. "I had two attempts," I said, "on the first one I told the crow your names and that you were in the far west, but I didn't get any response to that attempt. The second time I asked him to deliver it to you in Tir Na Nog, the 'Land of Youth'. That seemed to do the trick."

The pair of them sat and stared at me. "Amazing," said Cass.

I decided to change the subject because their joint gaze was getting a bit unsettling. "Do you think you'll be able to carry on with the Dolls House furniture now?" I asked.

Davi brightened at this and replied, "Yes, we can finish your furniture commission at long last, Mr Geoff. What was left? Just bunk beds with a ladder, and a double bed with bedside tables, I think. We can start on those this week and ask Catalina and Meg to run up the bed clothes for us."

I left them on that high note and thought I'd give them some time to settle down. I also thought about remuneration. They had spent their hacksaw silver first on Old Mother Airmid, then on Guthrum and his thugs. There couldn't be much if any silver left. I had a look online and settled on solid silver earrings, which you can buy quite cheaply, I found.

For Cass and Davi they'd have the same sort of feel as arm rings, which have always been used as money. I ordered four pairs, two each, of the chunkiest creole style ones I could find, and at least felt satisfied I could now pay them off and give them a thank you present. All was well with the world.

14. Call of the Woods

The following week Cassivellaunus and Davidillidallion proudly presented the last of the furniture. Mistresses Catalina and Meg had made beautiful little mattresses, pillows and bed clothes, and both the double bed and the bunk bed were little works of art in their own right. I said we should drink a toast to celebrate completion of the commission and fetched some egg cups and a bottle of port, which seemed to be the tipple of choice after mead. We sat in my workshop and toasted 'future collaborations', then sat companionably together, me on a chair and them on the handle of a hammer on my workbench.

"What will you do with the furniture now, send it to North Weald in a box again?" asked Cassivellaunus.

"Well actually," I replied, "the Covid restrictions have been relaxed a bit and I'm allowed to visit them, so long as we stay outside. I thought I'd check with Lorraine's friend, then drive over there soon and deliver them myself. It would be nice to see the furniture in the doll's house." They looked thoughtful about this, and Cass nodded slowly.

"Yes, it really would." he said. "Why don't we come with you?" This was something of a shock.

"Ummm," I said, "Isn't North Weald in a different kingdom or something?" Anyhow, I continued, "it would be a difficult journey for you."

"Oh, it would be difficult by hedgehog, certainly," said Davi, "but you'll be travelling in your motorised carriage, on men's roads, so it will be an easy journey. We could sit in the back."

This sounded so totally reasonable that I almost said, "Fine, tag along then," but managed to stop myself. "And what if someone sees you sitting in the back goggling out of the window?" I asked.

"I'd have the Highway Police all over me, and you two would end up in a display case somewhere."

"You forget that only your young can see us, generally, Mr Geoff," responded Davi, "and none of you believe them when they do in any case."

I cast my mind back to the Cottingley Fairies case and had to admit that this was about right. "Let me think on it," I said. "I'm not ruling it out, I just want to think it through."

Once alone I did just that. It was true that no one was likely to see them, and if they did, they'd probably dismiss it. If we got stuck in a traffic jam or something the lads would just have to put a blanket over their heads. Once we arrived in North Weald at the home of Lorraine's friend everyone would sit in the garden, so if I gave Cass and Davi precise instructions about where in the house the doll's house lived (i.e. the spare bedroom in the loft space) they could sneak inside (which I was sure they'd be good at) and take a good look.

I had to admit I did feel that they deserved a chance to see their work in its final setting, and they'd been through hell recently, so it would be an outing, a treat. So that was decided. I would just need to think of a clear signal for when it was time for them to get back to the car. I'd make some excuse to sound the horn, twice. That would cover it. All sorted then.

The next morning, I pottered down to the summer house to give Cass and Davi a bonus payment on completion of the commission. I'd taken them a creole earing each, and said, "I want to thank you both for finishing the whole huge job, and for your beautiful craftsmanship all the way through. I know you've been through some hard times, so I'd like to give you each a bonus." I handed over the earrings, which were super shiny and brand new, unlike the ancient pen which I had cut up to make my original hack saw silver.

They were both a little overwhelmed I think, but Cassivellaunus managed to say, "Thank you so much, Mr Geoff, you've paid us handsomely already, but this is a very welcome gift. We have had expenses!"

To get over this awkward moment I said, "I think the trip to North Weald will be possible after all. I've thought it through, and I think it could work," and I sat down on the veranda and explained the plan in detail.

When I was done, they were both beaming broadly.

"Excellent," said Davi. "We've already made preparations—we'll show you."

They hurried into their workshop and emerged with something in plain white timber which looked like a cross between a child seat and the bleachers at a baseball stadium.

"This can go in the back of your carriage so that we'll be high enough to see out," explained Davi.

I almost started to explain seat belt laws but thought better of it. No doubt they probably only applied to human beings anyway. They were clearly both pretty excited about the whole endeavour, and wanted to know how soon it would be, so I said I'd check with Lorraine's friend and let them know.

We agreed on the following Monday, when the weather looked promising, and Lorraine's friend and I would be able to sit in the garden for a chat. I told Cass and Davi that it would be in two days' time, and that I'd leave the back door of the car open so they could hide themselves inside until we were on the road. I said I'd put their car seat contraption in the back in advance. Come the day, all this went to plan. I headed for the A1 and the lads set up their bleachers on the back seat and sat goggling out of the window. I think they were a bit stunned by the speed of travel but spotted the river Lea as we passed over it and muttered suitable utterances of respect. We came off the motorway and drove towards North Weald on the Epping Road, through the dense old woodland which surrounds it.

As we drove Cassivellaunus and Davidillidallion chattered on about everything they could see from the back seat.

Suddenly Cass asked, "How does your carriage work, Mr Geoff, is it an enchantment?"

It looked like I had to try to explain internal combustion to two supernatural entities. "No, it's not magic at all," I said. "It's science. We drill for oil underground. It's a kind of carbon product, distilled from millions of ancient trees really. It's very flammable, so in the, er, carriage is an engine which uses it to make explosions." They looked around them and under the seat at this, so I continued, "it's perfectly safe. It all happens right at the front under the bonnet." I waved my hand in the direction of the engine.

"I see," said Davi, "just ahead of your groin then, you mean."

"Er, yes, I suppose so," I replied. "I'd never really thought about it."

Davi continued to muse on the phenomenon of motor vehicles. "But they're so poisonous," he said. "You can smell how poisonous the smoke that comes out of them is, and if you don't breathe it in, it goes into the air and poisons the sky instead. I don't understand why everybody seems to have one. Who forces you to use them?"

"No one forces us to use them," I responded. "Some people don't use them, or won't use them, but they're so convenient and people get such pleasure from them that nearly everyone *does* use them." They looked at each other long and hard at this, and Davi seemed genuinely puzzled.

"So", he said at last, "everyone knows that they're poisoning themselves and everything else in the world, every day, but they carry on anyway because they like the carriages, and because they're so handy. Is that about it?"

"Er, yes, I guess that's right." I had to admit. They didn't respond to this at all. I suppose there was nothing to be said, really. They sat back and watched the forest go by and I drove and brooded on the huge folly of mass consumption and surrender in the face of advertising.

We arrived in North Weald and parked up on the drive of the house. I'd explained to the lads where the doll's house was, and they understood that the humans would all be outside until I sounded the car horn. That was the signal to leg it back to the car, where they would find the rear door ajar.

"Thank you, Mr Geoff," beamed Davi. "We'll take care, and we'll be back as soon as you sound your horn. We can be near invisible when we put our minds to it!" and they were gone.

I greeted Lorraine's friend Catherine, said how good it was to be able to visit people again, then her little granddaughter Danni took my hand and we headed into the garden for tea and a chat. Hopefully Cassivellaunus and Davidillidallion had negotiated two flights of stairs and found their way to the loft conversion, the doll's house, and their furniture in its full glory. I hoped they wouldn't take offence at the fact that there would be dollies lounging all over it. I delayed handing over the box containing the little beds, which I'd left in the car. The last thing I wanted was for an excited Danni to rush off to put them in the bedroom and catch Cass and Davi red handed. I'd give them to her when I'd sounded the car horn and the coast was clear, I decided. The best laid plans of mice and men, however, are apt to go awry, and soon Danni declared that she was bored now, no thank you she didn't want another cake, and she was going indoors to play. I must have turned white because Catherine asked if I was OK and poured me more tea, but there wasn't much I could do except pray that the lads really were invisible. I should have known better I suppose.

We'd been catching up for a while and I was thinking about heading home when Danni came skipping out of the house for another cup cake.

"I've been playing with my doll's house," she declared. "The little men have been showing me how everything works, they're very clever. They're not very pretty though. Too hairy." She smiled delightedly at me.

"Don't they have wonderful imaginations at that age," said Catherine. "That old doll's house has provided hours of entertainment for her."

"Well Danni," I said, "I have two little beds for you, then your doll's house will be finished," I said. "Let's go to the car and fetch them."

We walked to the front of the house, and I got the furniture package from the back seat of the car, leaving the door open.

"Must test the horn before I start back," I said, lamely, and gave it two good toots. Catherine looked at me a bit sideways, but she'd probably discussed with Lorraine many times what a weirdo

I was, so didn't comment. We said our goodbyes and I allowed long enough for Cass and Davi to make it back to the car, then I started up, waved to Catherine and Danni and headed back towards Epping.

I checked in the rear view and thankfully there was Cass sitting on the bleachers and gazing unconcernedly out of the window.

"Where's Davidillidallion?" I asked.

"Oh," replied Cass, "he heard the call of the Wodewose, and he's gone into the woods." I nearly did an emergency stop in the middle of Epping High Street but managed to stay calm.

"What," I asked after a moment, "is a Wodewose?"

"Oh, he's the wild man of the woods," said Cassivellaunus. "A kind of hairy, naked man that lives deep in ancient woodland and avoids contact with your kind." *Like sasquatch*, then. I thought, but English.

"I don't mean that he literally heard the Wodewose calling to him, Mr Geoff." Explained Cass. It's a what we say when someone needs to go into the deep forest for a while and restore their energies.

Davidillidallion was very impressed with these old woodlands as we travelled to North Weald and decided on the way that he was going to spend time in them and revitalise his spirit." I thought about

141

'forest bathing' in Japan, 'Shinrin-Yoku', and the Scandinavian relationship with 'The Nature', and decided Davi was probably on some sort of forest spa retreat.

"Will he want us to pick him up later?" I asked.

"Oh no," replied Cassivellaunus, "he'll probably be a few days, and he'll make his own way back, of course, if he *does* encounter the Wodewose in the forest he might be much longer, they are ancient and very wise in the ways of the trees. There's a great deal a carpenter can learn from them."

It was all a bit unsettling, although Cassivellaunus didn't seem mildly concerned and chattered all the way home. I decided not to mention his encounter with Danni, since it all seemed to have gone remarkably well. I said goodbye to him at the summer house then headed indoors to report back to Lorraine on how Catherine was, and to look up Wodewose online. It seemed they first appeared in literature in Ancient Greece as long ago as 300 BC, and were presented as being human, but totally wild and very hairy, living in the deepest woods and avoiding mankind.

In medieval Switzerland peasants would try to trap them and only release them in exchange for their deep and mystical knowledge of the woods. Not exactly Bigfoot then, I thought, more a natural man with a deep affinity for trees.

Next day I went down the garden path for a chat with Cassivellaunus. He was quite unconcerned that Davi wasn't back, but I persevered and said, "Why don't we both drive over to Epping Forest and have a look around? We might bump into him or he might spot us. I'll take some sandwiches and my old hazel stick for poking about in the bushes." He seemed much more interested in the hazel stick than in Davi's welfare.

"Why hazel? Mr Geoff, if you don't mind me asking," he wanted to know.

I explained that I had made myself three walking sticks over the years, hazel, which was a symbol for wisdom for the celts, ash, which represented strength and courage for the Norse, and plum which has to do with love and protection.

He cocked his head on one side and gave me an appraising look.

"You never cease to amaze," he said. I explained that the hazel stick was special because of my long relationship with it.

"It's a long story," I said. "When my daughter and my son were little, we'd all been walking in the Chilterns in Bedfordshire, when I realised I'd stepped on a little seedling, a hazel only two or three inches high. It was right on the path and doomed to destruction, so I dug it up with my penknife, wrapped its roots in a wet tissue and popped it in my pack.

Back home I planted it at the bottom of my garden, a different garden to my current one, and it's still there, flourishing. I've coppiced it once or twice and made myself the hazel stick, and a similar one for a walking friend. The stick has accompanied me the length of Hadrian's wall and helped me over *The Stipperstones* in Shropshire in a couple of feet of snow. It's a good stick.

"I cut the ash stick in this garden," I continued, and it's seen me the length of St Cuthbert's way, from Melrose Abbey to Lindisfarne, finishing in the fudge shop there. Excellent!"

"The plum has only been pottering round Epping Forest so far, but I've got plans for it. The Ridgeway, perhaps."

When I'd finished, he continued looking at me strangely.

"May I see your sticks, Mr Geoff?" He asked, so I went back to the house to fetch them. They're all about a metre long, so were like scaffold poles to Cassivellaunus, but he examined them very thoroughly, pacing up and down the length of them as they lay on the grass.

"You've coated them with something but left the handles bare," he commented.

I nodded.

"That's right, I like to feel the wood, it connects you with the trail somehow." I explained.

When he'd finished, he sat down on the veranda and said, "The hazel one especially is quite magically charged. Either you've accidentally picked a plant with strong inherent earth magic, or you've unknowingly charged it through use. Either way it's quite potent. I'm truly surprised. I didn't think men still had it in them to do that, but some obviously still do. Perhaps we *could* take a walk through the woods, and I'll tell you a little about trees."

I smiled back and said, "I do know a little about trees, Cassivellaunus. I've studied them for years."

"Well," he responded, "I'll introduce you to some, then."

I took my old sticks back to the house with a new respect and planned a little expedition to the forest later in the week.

15. The wood for the trees

We fixed on Wednesday as the day for our forest walk, and set off nice and early for Epping, Cassivellaunus watching the world from his grandstand seat in the back. I had got out my old walking boots as the forest can be pretty muddy at times, and if you go off the trail it gets quite challenging. I took my old hazel stick for luck and put my battered OS Explorer 174 in my pack just in case. I always feel happier with a map in my pack. Cassivellaunus of course came just as he was, although I had a feeling, he was equipped for anything the woods could throw at him. I parked at the Epping end of the forest, and we headed down the Green Ride past Ambresbury Banks, which was an Iron Age fort, although it was probably used for corralling livestock in times of trouble, according to current thinking. We walked through Long Running, a clearing in the woods rich with gorse and ferns, pausing to gaze into the little pond in the middle where deer come to drink, and continued along the main trail through Great Monk Wood and Little Monk Wood. It was here that Cassivellaunus began my woodland education. I started it I suppose, by saying that they both had 'Monk Wood' in their names because Waltham Abbey had once owned the land and had exploited the beech trees for centuries. That was why the trees were coppiced, I explained.

They now grow in tangled misshapen forms, far removed from what a beech itself intends to look like. They are all knobbly buttresses and rounded haunches. When it rains their smooth grey bark looks like the slick skin of seals or sea monsters.

Cass listened with polite interest, then responded, "Actually they're not too fussed about what happens to their growth above ground, not compared with their roots under the ground. So long as they have a big enough spread of leaves to drink the light, and their boughs don't break in the gales, they're happy enough. They've grown to accept the grazing of animals and the hacking of men, and they live on in spite of it. These old, coppiced trees have accepted that they now have five or six trunks above man height, and they've carried on. They'll actually live longer than a tree left alone to live its natural life."

Oddly enough I remembered having read that coppiced trees often outlived natural specimens, so he seemed to know what he was talking about.

Cassivellaunus continued. "The roots are all joined up with special mould, that helps them talk to each other and feed other trees that are in trouble if they need to. It's like one of your towns, with all sorts of trades and deals going on, except that it's underground and men can't see it, so they don't think about it. I'll bet you have always thought of a tree as a tall trunk with leaves on top, Mr Geoff."

He smiled up at me. I nodded and said that humans usually do think of trees that way, yes. Ask any child to draw a tree and that's what you'll get. I was thinking about what Cass had said. He was referring to mycorrhizal fungi which grow around and into the roots of trees and connect them. Apparently, it is now thought that they allow the exchange of sugars, and information about predators and pests. The fungus specific to birch is the marvellous bright red, white spotted fly agaric, the classic toadstool of folklore. I'd seen a few in Epping Forest in Autumn.

I very nearly said to Cass that if we found one, he'd have to sit on it and pose for a photo, but I thought better of it. We walked on as far as Loughton Camp, another Iron Age fort, and found a log to sit on for lunch.

I took a sandwich out of my pack and cut off a portion for Cass, who cut it into smaller portions and munched contentedly, gazing into the trees.

"What do you think our chances of finding Davidillidallion today are?" I asked.

"None at all, to be honest, Mr Geoff," he replied immediately. "He'll have gone right off of any path into the deepest woods, where he can talk to the oldest trees. He'll have been foraging for food and drink for a few days now and sleeping in a handmade shelter. If he did find a Wodewose, and if its approachable, it might have allowed him inside the spirit of the wood, inside the mind of the wood, if you like. That's what we all hope to be able do at some point in our time in this world."

It dawned on me that Davi hadn't just wandered off into the woods on some sort of elfin jolly. He was on a pilgrimage, hoping to find himself in the woods. It was probably only right and proper to give him time and space, and it would definitely be quite wrong to go crashing about in the understorey shouting out his name, as though I was looking for a lost dog (which I had considered doing). This was less of a forest spa retreat and more of a life changing experience, I now realised.

"How will he get back when he's done?" I asked, ever one to worry about the details.

"Hedgehog, probably." Replied Cass, unconcernedly. "Although he might be able board a boat on the Lea and come back via the Thames and the Brent. Less fleas that way."

It seemed that we had exhausted the subject of Davidillidallion's welfare. We didn't know where he was, how he'd get back or how long he'd be. That was about it, then.

"Let's go back through the woods," said Cassivellaunus brightly when we'd finished lunch.

"I thought we were in the woods?" I said lamely, which elicited a broad smile.

"Oh no," he said, "we've just been on man paths. I'll show you the *woods*, Mr Geoff."

We headed from Loughton camp north and west, towards the field centre. Off of the beaten path there were plenty of obstacles, a lot of them to do with holly. Holly forms the understory of these old beech woods, along with yew, and it gets pretty dense in some areas. I had taken shortcuts between paths before, so wasn't too surprised by the terrain, although I had to do longer detours around fallen trees and holly clumps than Cassivellaunus did.

He often simply walked right under fallen trees or right through the middle of a dense thicket. He seemed to have a natural instinct for a clear path through these hazards. What *did* surprise me was that he kept up a near constant dialogue with the trees as we passed them, commenting on the weather, complimenting them on their healthy appearance or commenting on their surrounding neighbours.

"Cassivelaunus, when you talk to the trees like that, do you hear any reply?" I asked.

"Of course, Mr Geoff," he replied. "They are alive, you know, and aware that we're here. It's a sort of group awareness though, not like ours. I think all of them together, joined up below ground as a sort of community, have an awareness much bigger than a tree on its own. That's why it's so sad when men plant one tree, decide they've done it a massive favour by letting it live at all, and leave it to live out its years alone."

This gave me food for thought. Over the years I'd planted plenty of trees and thought myself very noble for doing so, but they'd always been lone specimens. I don't think I've ever planted a group of trees together.

"So, what sort of answers do you get, Cassivellaunus?" I asked.

"You don't hear them with your ears like speech, Mr Geoff," he said. "You get a feeling, an emotion, it's as though you tune in to what they're experiencing. And then sometimes, from a big old mother tree that's been rooted in the same place for centuries, you might get a really clear message, but not in words. More like a clear idea in your head."

My expression must have said that I didn't follow this at all, because Cassivellaunus sat down on a big old root and tried again.

"When we cut timber for furniture, we look for a branch that might have grown away from the light or been masked by other trees. A branch that the tree might be able to afford to lose. We always tell the tree what we want the wood for, and we never cut down a whole tree, like men do. If we get a strong feeling of objection, we don't cut at all. Because we try to be considerate the forest is more sympathetic to us and tolerates us better than it does men. That's why you're afraid in the forest after dark, Mr Geoff, and I'm not. You can feel the animosity of the trees, they're talking to you."

"I think I see," I said slowly, "humans have evolved away from woodland life for centuries, so we've lost the understanding we once had, and don't hear the messages even though we might still receive them."

"Exactly right," he beamed. "You're part of the living world like everything else, but your record is so bad that the trees have come to distrust and fear your kind." *Great*, I thought, I'm one of the pariah species, the only one out of them all to fear and mistrust.

"Hold on though," I said, "what about Master Feller Bellerkind?" He doesn't sound like he's too fussy about what he cuts down."

"There are always exceptions which prove the rule Mr Geoff," He replied, "but even he tends to choose trees which are least viable. I tell you what," he continued brightly, "I'll introduce you to a tree I know. Who knows, you might get on really well together." He stood and continued through the woodland with me trailing thoughtfully behind him.

Davidillidallion was watching in complete stillness and silence from deep within the dusty darkness of a yew thicket.

When we'd passed and disappeared into the woods, he said to the Wodewose, "Do you think I should have called out and told them all was well?"

"No," the Wodewose replied, inside his head. "All is well and there is nothing to fear. Let them continue on their way and we shall go on ours."

Cassivellaunus and I continued through the forest, bypassing the field centre and passing Wake Valley Pond on our right. It was a mellow autumn day with sun and cloud, fairly dry underfoot, and quite mild, so very pleasant for walking. We crossed Sunshine Plain keeping north of the Epping Road. Cassivellaunus continued his woodland lecture on the history of humans and the woods.

"The problems began as soon as men settled down and began building homes together, which was a very long time ago now. They cut down trees to form clearings and to use as building material and for fires. They quickly began to see the woods as a place to go to for timber whenever they wanted it, and probably never dreamed that it could ever run out or be destroyed. In time there was a clear difference in their minds between the men's towns, where they were in control, and the wild woods, where they definitely weren't. This became a fear and even a hatred of the woods, so that by the time the monks and their churches came along, men were taught that the woods were evil, the home of spirits and monsters.

Slowly, slowly the men cut down nearly all the trees in Albion, to make houses and especially to make longbows, and then ships. By the time of your great British Navy, your 'Hearts of Oak', there were only little patches of woodland left, and most of the country was turned over to meadowland for sheep and cattle, or else great fields of wheat and barley."

I thought it might be good to get a word in here, so I said. "It's true that our forefathers exploited the woods Cassivellaunus, and I know that English yew nearly went extinct because of the longbow industry, but we understand the need for trees better now. We know that there would be no breathable atmosphere without enough trees, and a lot of people plant trees to try and create new woodland parks for people to visit and learn about nature."

He nodded at this and replied, "It's still all about you though, isn't it? 'How shall we breathe, where shall our children go for a walk, what if we're killing trees that we might be able to use for medicine'. What you have probably never thought about, Mr Geoff, is that, as men spread their towns across the land, the folk who had lived there forever were forced into the places where men didn't go, and those places were the woods. The monks were probably right. The ancient woods are sanctuaries for old Gods, creatures like the Wodewose, and for the folk. There's nowhere else for them to go, unless it's the rivers and the mountains, and they're a bit extreme for me, I can tell you." This was an eye opener, I had to admit.

While I was pondering this Cassivellaunus continued, "The most ancient tree in Albion is in the Pict's lands which you call Perthshire. It's a yew tree which is about 3000 years old. That means it sprung from a seed when men were still making their tools from bronze. It's witnessed the men of Rome come and go, and everything that's passed since." I thought I knew what was coming next. He was talking about the Fortingall yew, which I'd read about before. "Do you know what 'oh so considerate men' are doing to it now, Mr Geoff?" He continued, "they're pulling branches off of it for good luck keepsakes. It's beginning to die because men think its age makes it lucky, and that's my point, I suppose. Even when men sense the power of something, they destroy it for their own selfish ends. You need to learn to respect the other lives that you share the land with, before you kill everything, and then yourselves."

We walked on in thoughtful silence, focussed on the thick mat of golden leaves underfoot. Cassivellaunus stopped at the foot of an old, coppiced beech, and eyed its canopy.

"This is a mother tree, Mr Geoff," he said. "Although that's a misleading name really, because beech has both male and female flowers, but it does nurture and watch over the young beech trees growing around it, feeding them and giving them water through the root system in times of need."

He stepped up onto the gnarly root bole and gently laid one palm flat on the bark, closing his eyes and breathing shallowly. After a while he stepped back and said, "I've tried to explain that you're interested, and that you're not hostile. Do as I did, and ask the beech a question, then listen carefully for the response, or really feel for it, if you see what I mean." I hesitated at this, what do you ask a tree, if you're beginning to suspect that it might somehow understand you, and *may* even reply?

Eventually I'd formulated a question that seemed sensible enough, so I stood closer, placed a palm flat on the cool, smooth bark and closed my eyes. I thought as clearly as I could, "Is my friend Davidillidallion Hollyfoot safe in these woods?"

Then I stood waiting, still touching the bark, increasingly thinking that nothing was happening. Maybe I had a feeling that I was getting the message, "safe and well. Learning, growing." Maybe I was imagining it though, the way thoughts intrude when you're trying to meditate. Certainly, there was no ethereal voice in my head, but I did continue thinking, "safe and well. Learning and growing." After a while I removed my hand and stepped back from the tree. I did feel calmer and less worried for Davi if nothing else. "Thank you, beech," I said, as we set off again towards Epping.

"Good," said Cassivellaunus. "That's a beginning, Mr Geoff. Practice it with the trees in your garden, respect them and get to know them."

We drove home uneventfully, in my case turning over a lot of thoughts about woods, trees, understanding and the nature of life generally. In Cass' case there was a lot going past the window which needed continuous study. We said our farewells at the summer house, and I headed indoors to tell the girls that I'd had a nice walk in the woods.

The next morning, I headed out early to exercise in the garden, and stopped by my favourite birch. It's a bit special because I found it as a seedling growing in a flowerpot with some geraniums. I couldn't tell what species it was from its seed leaves, but I *could* see that it planned on being a tree, so I re-potted it in a bigger container and watered it all summer. It soon revealed its true colours and the next year I planted it in the garden. A few years on and it's an elegant fifteen foot adult, with peeling silver bark, and catkins in spring. Birch is a fast developer. I stopped next to it and stepped off the path so that I could stand close enough to touch the bark. Placing my hand against it I closed my eyes and thought, "You are welcome here. You are safe." After a while I moved on, wondering if I could get away with planting a couple more birch next to it. Probably not. Mind you, who knows what sort of relationship it might have with the cherry and the plum trees either side of it? Now there's a thought!

Most days I stopped to make time for the local trees. There was a big old yew which was probably older than the house in whose garden it stood, and I gave it a nod and thought, "Good health," as I passed it on my walks. One local front garden had a little group of five birch trees, which I was now always pleased to see, and it occurred to me that the street trees, which were all London plane, probably had a root network all of their own, intermingling with the utility's trenches under the road. I may not have actually spoken with trees like Cassivellaunus did, but I certainly had a much greater awareness of them now and had learned to view them as fellow travellers on the planet rather than just useful plants. It was, as Cass had said, a beginning.

I'd looked up all I could find about the Wodewose, which to be honest wasn't much. The Wodewose appeared in the mythology of most European countries, as a vague man (or woman) of the woods, wild and hairy and generally alien. There were instances of them being captured, and sometimes being held so as to learn their wisdom.

I decided to sit down with Cassivellaunus sometime and find out what he thought they were, and just what Davidillidallion was up to. I caught Cass sitting on the summer house veranda one evening and joined him there, asking, "How are you coping without Davidillidallion? When do you think he'll be back?"

"I'm managing just fine thank you, Mr Geoff," he responded.

"There's not much work on at the moment, so Davidillidallion has picked a good time for his blossoming. I'm pleased for him." I thought on this for a moment, then said, "I don't really understand what's happening with Davidillidallion, or what this Wodewose is, or any of it really, Cassivellaunus. Please can you explain to me?"

He nodded at that, and said, "I'll fetch the mead."

Hunkered down in the dusk, among the wakening night-time sounds and smells of the garden, we sat cradling a little cup of old *Cat's Eye* each, and Cass began his explanation.

"The Wodewose come from the dawn of man when men first walked this land. Most men started to learn to make and use tools, build homes and hunt animals. Eventually they learned to farm crop plants, and the rest is history. There were some who didn't, though. They rejected stone tools and wooden shelters, they never wore clothes or grew crops. They were men, but they went off on a totally different path to the rest of you, and they've grown in very different ways through the many years since."

"All right" I said, "so they diverged in prehistory and they're still living out there in the deepest woods. Is that what you're saying, Cassivellaunus?"

He nodded and confirmed, "Yes, more or less, There's more to it than that though. They never used their minds for hunting or warfare or making more and more complicated machines like you do. They remained sensitive to the animals and plants around them. They lived in the woods like any other beast of the woods, aware of the seasons and other animals, and especially aware of the trees. Men are clever, whatever else they might be, and the Wodewose are men, just very different men.

Their cleverness though is all bound up in understanding the woods and the trees that form it." This really was food for thought. Cass was describing a divergent human population whose whole evolution had been focussed on woodland living. It was hard to believe they were to be found in Essex though.

"But, what about Davidillidallion?" I asked. "What is this 'blossoming' that you mentioned, and what exactly is he doing out there in the woods?" Cassivellaunus looked thoughtful for a while.

"That has a lot more to do with the ways of the folk," he said eventually, "and there are some things I can't tell you, no offence, Mr Geoff." He twiddled his beard bead between finger and thumb. Which I'd learned was usually a symptom of stress. "Think of it this way," he continued. "Most of the folk work very hard and have full lives, and very long lives too."

Unless their name is Pandemonious Balker, I thought, but I said nothing.

Cass continued, "There comes a time in most of our lives when we feel that we've moved too far from the magic which is our birth right. Too wrapped up in the everyday business of getting through life. That's when some of the folk decide to go into the woods, on their own, to relearn the natural magic of the world, to 'blossom anew', as the folk say. If you are lucky enough to find a

Wodewose who will teach you and steer you, it can be a life changing experience. You come back to the folk changed, more in tune with the magic of the land. I can't really tell you any more than that, Mr Geoff." He took a swig of old *Cat's Eye* and had clearly told as much as he was prepared to.

"So," I said tentatively, "perhaps Davidillidallion was so uncomfortable with the whole Pandemonious Balker affair that it set him thinking about going back to the woods, going out there and 'blossoming.' Do you think that might be it?"

Cassivellaunus smiled ruefully. "I think that's exactly it, Mr Geoff. I think he was disgusted by the whole business, but too loyal to object. I really hope everything works out for him in the woods."

We sat in silence for a while. I'd finished my little cup of mead, and it was almost dark, so I said, "I'm sure it *will* all work out, Cassivellaunus. We'll have to wait and see, but I've got faith in Davidillidallion, and you. Let's see what tomorrow brings—Good Night."

"Thank you, Mr Geoff," he said, "and a good night to you."

16. Return of the sage

There was no sign of Davidillidallion returning for some weeks, and life settled into a pattern without him. Cassivellaunus was around, working on whatever projects he had in hand, although I wasn't sure how well business had picked up for him since the banishment debacle. Autumn was definitely here, and the trees were shedding their leaves, so there was a great deal of sweeping and composting to be done outside.

It was in late October when I went outside one morning and immediately spotted a little green flag fluttering from the summer house. I hurried down the garden to tap on the shiny green door, which was now there for me continuously, although no one else ever seemed to notice it. Cass answered and came outside, quietly shutting the door behind him. He signalled that I should follow him and walked across to the other side of the garden where we both sat on the rockery stones.

"Good morning, Mr Geoff," he said, "Davidillidallion is back, he's in the workshop." I jumped up beaming like an idiot, but he raised his hand and continued, "sit down please, Mr Geoff. I need to explain some things to you." He sat in thoughtful silence for a while, then continued. "He has indeed blossomed, Mr Geoff. He *did* meet a Wodewose, and he's spent all this time living in the woods and learning its secrets. He's truly been very lucky, but he is changed, you'll find him quite different. I think it will be a while until he adjusts to living back among the folk again. Don't be offended, but can I ask you to wait for, perhaps, a fortnight, before you see him? Some of the folk will want to spend time with him and share his experiences."

I didn't think there was much choice to be honest, so I agreed without fuss to come back in a fortnight and see how Davi was doing. The days passed slowly, and I found myself gazing down the garden quite often. I have to admit that I was more than a little keen to see what changes his weeks in the woods had wrought on him, not to mention finding out all about the Wodewose. Because I was often glancing down to the summer house, I noticed Mistresses Catalina and Meg visiting, and on another day Thorfinn Thorfinnson and his mate Martin. What really got my attention though was the sight of Old Mother Airmid appearing out of the bushes and hobbling across the veranda to knock on the green door. I'd got the impression from Davidillidallion that she was a highly respected little old lady who was in very high demand for her healing and hexing services, so to see her fitting a visit to Davi into her busy schedule was impressive. There were other folk too, whom I didn't recognise, and it began to dawn on me that our Davi had become the local guru.

Then eventually Cassivellaunus raised the flag to signal a meeting, and I met him at the summer house. "I think it's a good time for you to meet Davidillidallion now, Mr Geoff," he said. "All the local folk have been to visit him, and we've even had folk from as far away as the valleys of the Great Ouse and the Nene, and a party from the Greensand Ridge in the county of Bedford, can you believe! Things have quietened down now though, so come with me and you can talk with him." He opened the green door and walked inside, and I heard Davi's voice, the same as it ever was, saying, "come inside, Mr Geoff," so I stepped through the doorway and stood looking around the workshop.

I'd never been inside before, so it was fascinating to see the tool racks and workbench up close. My subconscious was shouting what's wrong with this picture, idiot' and with a horrible jolt I realised that I was suddenly the same size as Cassivellaunus and Davi and was *inside* their other-dimensional workshop.

"How did that happen?" I said out loud and looked around to find Davidillidallion. He was sitting on a grand wooden chair with something of the throne about it, which was no doubt how he'd been receiving his many visitors. His face looked the same, but there was certainly something very different about his manner and the way he met my gaze with a cool, confident stare. I took a minute to examine him in detail. His old rusty brown and moss green work clothes had been replaced by a leaf green outfit which looked brand new, *probably a gift from Mistresses Catalina and Meg*, I thought.

His hair and beard were combed out and tied in neat ponytails, back and front respectively, and the stripey tasselled hat was gone entirely.

"It's good to see you again, Mr Geoff," he began. "It's good to be back in the workshop too, although my time in the woods was marvellous and I didn't want it to end."."

"It's good to see you too, Davidillidallion," I managed. "It's really weird to just walk into your workshop like this though. Before I was never totally sure whether it was really here or not."

He smiled at this and seemed suddenly much more like his old self. "You are a friend, Mr Geoff, and now I'm able to, I thought I'd ask you inside as a friend should."

I thought of my previous shrinking experiences, and said, "But I thought you had to get Mistress Catalina to do the laying on of hands and magic spells to shrink me before—I never just walked in like this."

"I used to, Mr Geoff, yes, "he replied, smiling more broadly, "but now I don't need to any more. I've learned a great deal and understood things much better now." *Cassivellaunus had been right*, I thought. This was going to take a bit of adjusting too. I sat down on a little stool and smiled back at Davi.

"I like the throne!" I said, as an icebreaker. "I'm glad," he replied, "Cassivellaunus made it for me while I was away. He knew I'd receive lots of visitors when I came back, and it was his gift to me."

Davidillidallion's throne

I decided to dive in at the deep end, so I took a deep breath and asked, "Can you tell me about what happened to you?" And so, he began to try to explain his transformation.

"When I headed into the woods on the day when we visited the doll's house in north Weald, I didn't have any clear idea or plan, except that the trees seemed very welcoming, and I needed to spend some time there. I told Cassivellaunus that I was heading into the woods for a while, and said I'd seek out a Wodewose to teach me, although I was half joking, really. I made a shelter under some dense holly, and foraged for blackberries, fungus and seeds. There was clean enough water to drink from the streams and ponds. I hadn't taken any tools with me, I didn't have my axe, just my belt knife, so I wasn't really prepared, but I got by all right, I lit a fire and kept it burning, and it was dry enough to be comfortable. I talked to plenty of old trees and felt I was a bit more settled in my mind, when early one day I walked right into a Wodewose. I'm still not sure whether I surprised him or whether he wanted me to see him, but I kept still and thought welcoming thoughts, and he didn't disappear into the trees." I rearranged myself on my stool and Davi stopped, to see if I had any questions, I think.

"What was it like, the Wodewose?" I asked, a bit lamely.

"Man sized, hairy all over, with long reddish-brown hair, but it was the eyes that struck me," replied Davi. "They were deeply thoughtful and very clever looking, and he never took them off of me. When he spoke to me, he didn't move his mouth, but I sort of felt his words in my head, if you know what I mean."

I shook my head, "I'm sorry, Davidillidallion, but I don't, really. I can't imagine what that must have been like," I said.

"I got used to it," he continued, "and found myself answering him without words, in fact. He said he could feel that I was trying to understand the essence of the trees, and that he would help me, if I wanted his help. Well, I said I did, very much, and we spent several days walking through the woods, talking with the trees, or really with the root-mind of the forest, I suppose. It's all one being you see, like an ant hill. You can't really speak to one tree separately unless it's growing totally on its own."

I nodded some more and let him continue.

"I learned a lot from my time with the Wodewose, among the trees. It's hard to explain to others though. I've been trying to tell the folk about it for days now, but I'm not sure I make myself clear. What you learn from trees is that there's one big awareness, Mr Geoff. There's actually one big mind and all living things are part of it, but nearly all the folk, and certainly all men, have lost touch with it. The Wodewose taught me to find that mind, that awareness, again, and to understand that all the everyday worries and concerns we have are just passing clouds. Life itself should be the real focus for us, not the living of it. Does that make any sense to you, Mr Geoff?"

I took a moment to digest this. "Yes, it does, Davidillidallion," I eventually replied. "Humans have similar ideas about awareness, and a bigger mind outside their own. It's one of the great mysteries of all time for us though, no one has ever been able to agree on the right way to understand it."

He nodded thoughtfully at this. "I hope to help all the folk here to understand it, Mr Geoff, and to change their lives once they do. I think that's all I can do."" It felt as though my audience was over, and I had been given plenty to think on.

"Thank you, Davidillidallion," I said. "You've explained what happened very well I think, and you've given me much to think about." I gave him a little bow, since it seemed appropriate somehow, and headed out of the workshop, immediately assuming my proper stature as I did so. That was a deeply weird experience, I thought, and it will take a little while to come to terms with it.

My friend the local carpenter has become Mahatma Hollyfoot, but there was certainly something in what he said.

Cassivellaunus came to see me a couple of days later. That's not such a simple exercise as it sounds. He was hanging around on the top patio outside the house when I went out in the morning, he'd probably been loitering there since dawn, waiting for me. He made little 'psss' noises until I noticed him, then beckoned me over to my workshop where there was a bit of privacy. I knelt down to better hear what was up, and he began.

"Er, I hope you're not offended, Mr Geoff, but someone special is coming to see Davidillidallion today, and it would be better if you weren't around when they did." Was that all?

I smiled and said, "Of course not Cassivellaunus. Is it a VIP, or royalty perhaps?"

"Er not exactly," he replied, looking a bit shifty. "It's Master Feller Bellerkind. Only he's always had, *difficulties* with men, let's say. Probably better just to keep out of the way. I'll put the green flag up when the coast is clear."

"No problem Cassivellaunus," I said, "I've got things indoors to keep me busy. When is he coming?"

"Oh soon, very soon, Mr Geoff," he responded. "That's why I've been getting in a bit of a state hanging around trying to catch you outside. I'd better be going, then. See you later." With that he was off through the flower bed and down to the summer house.

This gave me food for thought. The Master Feller had always been on the periphery of Cass and Davi's society, as far as I could gather. Semi wild, even. The fact that he'd sought an audience with Davi to seek his 'wisdom of the woods' was very impressive. I decided I had to have a peek at this, even if it meant hiding in the conservatory with my binoculars, so I went and fetched them and hunkered down where I had a good view of the bottom of the garden.

Soon enough Cassivellaunus appeared on the veranda and crossed to the seat in the corner of the garden, where the bamboo was thick and high. He disappeared between the shoots but soon returned, accompanied by the Master Feller. I adjusted my focus to get a better look. He was pretty impressive! Twice the height of Cass and Davi, he was as broad as he was tall, with a huge mane of reddish hair and a massive jutting beard. He moved awkwardly out in the open, and I could sense he was used to the deep cover of the woods and neglected areas where no human ventured. His clothes were more or less camouflage green and brown. The most striking features about him were his amazing hair and the large, polished axe at his belt. That was until he turned to look my way, mind you, and then I decided that his eyes were his outstanding feature. Wide, staring eyes under a beetling brow, they looked quite mad.

He ambled to the conservatory veranda and somehow disappeared through the little door, which was half his height, in much the same way as I had done, I supposed.

Time elapsed, then eventually the door opened, and Cass stuck his head out to take a look around, then beckoned Bellerkind outside. The two of them ambled to the bamboo corner, said a few words, and then the Master Feller disappeared between the shoots and was gone. To be honest, I hoped never to see him again. He'd had an edgy, feral feel about him that was really unsettling. I gave it an hour or so, then wandered down the garden path to sate my curiosity. If I'm honest I was bursting to know what had been said, and how the Master Feller received it. I was wondering if I'd be shrunk and invited inside again, but this time the carpenters came outside to meet me, and we sat on the veranda again just like old times.

Master Feller Bellerkind

"So, how did it go?" I asked after a couple of minutes of quiet contemplation had passed.

"It went well, I think." Davidillidallion responded. "He definitely wanted to know everything the Wodewose had to say. He seems to have a deep respect for them."

"More than he has for anything else," put in Cassivellaunus.

Davi gave him a look, then continued. "I tried to explain that it was wrong for him to harm other creatures for his own pleasure, that he could live well from his labours, and that the folk were beginning to value him as a reliable timber supplier, so he should build on that.""

I nodded and asked, "How did he react to that, then?"

"Well," said Davi, "he promised to quit hanging around under bridges, waiting for people to cross them. Says he hasn't done it for centuries anyway, not since men stopped driving their animals over them." It looked like Davi might be *on his way to saving a sinner*, I thought. His time in the woods had obviously brought *some* payback.

"He didn't kill anyone or break anything," said Cassivellaunus brightly, "so I think that was a good outcome, don't you?" We both nodded thoughtfully. "We're going to the forest for a while," broke in Cassivellaunus. "I want to experience what Davidillidallion has been telling me about for myself. I think he can explain the root-mind of the woods better to me while we're there and help me to hear it for myself. We'll be away for a while, so we'll shut up the workshop while we're gone and put it about that we're both going to be away."

I gave this a bit of thought before I responded. "Do you feel that you should be living in the woods, rather than here in the city, Davidillidallion?" I asked. "Tell me honestly, please. I'd really like to know."

He smiled at this and replied, "Of course I do, Mr Geoff, but all the folk we work with are here along the Brent valley, its where our trade is. It would be an upheaval to move everything out to the forest." They had worked here for a long, long time I reflected. Probably longer than I realised. Nevertheless, Davidillidallion had changed, changed fundamentally, so perhaps now was the time to make a move and go through that upheaval. I'd wait until they'd been on their forest retreat and see how things stood then, I decided.

17. Savings Account

Cassivellaunus and Davidillidallion set off early one morning in late October, locking up the workshop and dissolving the doorway before commanding the heavily laden hedgehogs' 'mush' and heading off into the bamboo thicket, North and Westward. I'd offered them a lift to North Weald, but they had said thank you, but they'd rather make their own way, at their own pace. It was all a bit sad really, but they were doing what they'd long wanted to, and what they'd decided on.

They said they were leaving the bulk of their tools and their best quality timber in the workshop, and only taking the essentials for a stay in the woods, although those amounted to two full hedgehog howdahs. Clearly, they'd be back though, so I settled down to a quiet winter and tried to forget about them. Christmas came and went, as it does, with weeks of anticipation and preparation, a few days of festivities, then a deflated feeling to take us into the New Year.

Lorraine had a call in January from her friend Catherine in North Weald. Apparently one of Catherine's friends had seen the doll's house and its furniture at Christmas and fallen in love with it. She had a daughter of her own, and a wealthy husband who ran his own company, and who was apparently prepared to pay whatever was necessary to procure his daughter a full set of similarly beautiful furniture.

"What an opportunity," said Lorraine brightly. "You love making that stuff, and you've been spending hours in the workshop, so it's ideal, really. I've got to admit you're really good at it, although God forbid I should feed your ego! Everyone should be happy." *Possibly not*, I thought. Certainly not me! No way could I replicate Cass and Davi's work, certainly not to a standard to match little Danni's furniture.

This was a dilemma because I had no idea when the lads would be back, so I couldn't even make up an excuse for delay. I got round it by saying that I'd be in touch and start work when I was able to take on the whole commission, which would buy me some time. Then I set about anxiously checking the summer house for signs of life. It had occurred to me while I was waiting for news that Epping Forest probably wasn't the ideal place for members of the folk to go on retreat. I knew it quite well, and knew it was thronged with people and their dogs, and horses, especially on fine days.

People penetrated into even the deepest woods at times, and precious little of it was unexplored. How the Wodewose had survived undetected I couldn't begin to imagine, although I suspected it was something to do with having a multi-dimensional existence, much like the workshop in my summer house. This got me thinking about better alternatives, and the idea of a small, private wood began to germinate. I did a little online research and found that it was possible to buy the freehold on a one acre or maybe a one-and-a-half-acre wood for around 20,000, depending on where you were looking. Wouldn't it be wonderful if the lads could move into their own undisturbed woodland, and it would be pretty wonderful to be able to carve my own spoons there every now and then, too! A woodland retreat that we could control the use of, and a sanctuary from the world. I filed the idea away for future reference.

It wasn't until early March that I had any word from Cassivellaunus and Davidillidallion, by which time I was considering buying the very best dolls house furniture I could find online and selling it on to Catherine's friend at a loss. A crow caught my attention by cawing continuously while I was trying to do my Ba Duan Jin outside. Outdoor exercise in cold, wet weather is challenging and takes a bit of perseverance, so I ignored him for a while until I realised, he wasn't going to go away. I gave him my undivided attention and he glided onto the grass and waddled up to me to present his message. This was in a little metal cylinder like the previous one I'd received, and I carefully relieved the crow of it, then went indoors to fetch him a reward. He headed into the treeline to devour his sausage, and I headed into my workshop, filled with excitement to see what the message was.

'Dear Mr Geoff,

Greetings from the woods from your friends Cassivellaunus and Davidillidallion. We have had an interesting time among the trees and have spent the winter garnering our strength, as do they. We have both learned much, and Cassivellaunus is now satisfied that he understands the life of the trees better. We plan to head back to our old workshop in the next few days, and shall see you then, so please don't trouble to send a reply (although I am sure you are able)!

Your friend

Davidillidallion Hollyfoot'

I read through it again and thought 'Gods be praised. I just hope they're up for some full-on carpentry when they get back.'

Sure, enough two days later the little green door had reappeared in my summer house and having waited till the next day to allow them time to settle in, I headed outside to greet the lads. They were both in fine spirits and were in the process of setting up the workshop again, so their time away didn't seem to have changed them beyond all recognition. They looked fit and well and were certainly more tanned than when I had last seen them, and thankfully Davi seemed less thoughtful and much more his old self. They told me they'd set up a camp in the deepest woodland they could find, although people had come trooping through occasionally, even in winter, and dogs were a constant nuisance, although generally friendly.

"It's a pity that men can't experience the outdoors without having to dominate it," said Cass, "The car parks, the dogs and horses everywhere, if only you could see yourselves as part of the whole web of life and act accordingly, it would be a lot easier!"

This seemed like too good an opportunity to waste, so I seized the moment and said, "I've been thinking about how people dominate the land, actually, Cassivellaunus. I've done some research while you've been away, and found that you can buy a small woodland, not too far away, and actually own it, so that you can decide how you want it used, and who goes there when. It is quite an expensive proposition though." I waited for a reaction. They looked long and hard at each other. I think the concept of actually owning land themselves had never occurred to either of them (although the grand duke had been pretty clear about exiling them from his patch)!

Eventually Cassivellaunus said, "That's a very interesting idea, Mr Geoff, I think Davidillidallion, and I need to talk about it, and think it over for a while." Davi nodded thoughtfully, so I dropped the subject and asked them about life in the woods. We talked for a good long while about camping among the trees, hunting for your dinner with a longbow, and sleeping under the stars, and when I left them, I had a definite hankering for the outdoor life.

Cassivellaunus hunting

Next time we met up at the bottom of the garden I told them that, if they wanted it, I had a lucrative contract for more dolls house furniture from someone who had seen their work and greatly admired it. This was well received, in fact Cass said it was precisely what they needed to focus them on work again. Excellent! I said I'd get a list of precisely what the requirements were, and they said they'd start sourcing timber for the job, so all seemed well after all. Finally, I was able to go back to Catherine in North Weald, apologise for being so busy for so long, and offer to start her friend's project as soon as she gave me a list of furniture. Phew!

Work started up within a few days, with the hated sawpit back in use, and discreet stacks of drying planks appearing in a corner of the summer house. I was admiring the first completed item, a chest of drawers, when out of the blue Cassivellaunus said, "Davidillidallion and I have thought long and hard about buying a wood, Mr Geoff, and we both think it's an excellent idea. We'd move our operation there, and live there too, which we both feel would be the right thing to do now. Would you be willing to help us with the process of buying it, though? We can hardly roll up to the owner's house and knock on his door!" I was a bit taken aback by this, although I had introduced the idea, so I suppose shouldn't have been.

I managed to say, "I'm really pleased Cassivellaunus, I'd be happy to deal with the mechanics of the purchase, it's not quite a matter of going to see the owner I'm afraid. But have you both thought about the cost, I wonder? We're talking about around £20,000 in men's money, which is a *lot* of silver."

He smiled a bit slyly at this, I thought, and replied, "I don't think that will be a problem, Mr Geoff, to be honest. Davidillidallion and I have resources, we have funds at our disposal, you know."

I nodded and said, "OK, that's good, but they'd have to be *liquid* funds that we could use in the purchase, actual money, you know." This didn't seem to throw him, in fact he seemed even more cocksure, and just said, "I tell you what, we'll show you."

We parted without him disclosing what it was they were actually going to show to me however, and I decided to lay some groundwork for the possibility of buying some woodland. After dinner I explained to Linda and Lorraine that some wood-carving friends of mine were considering buying a small wood to manage and to use for weekend breaks and little holidays away from it all. As it happened, I had a savings bond which was maturing soon, and Lorraine agreed that investing some of the proceeds in land was probably a wise move. She used to be a banker before we retired, and she is still very good at it!

Next time I met Cassivellaunus and Davidillidallion they announced that we would take a walk at dusk that evening, and that they would show me something which might surprise me. They both had a certain swagger about them, and I just had to find out what this was all about, so I met them at the bottom of the garden as soon it was getting dark. They'd told me to dress for the outdoors and wear my boots, so I was pretty much kitted up for a country walk.

"Walk with us, Mr Geoff," intoned Davi, and I found myself their size without any noticeable change occurring.

His powers were certainly not diminishing with time! We headed into the bamboo and through a suspiciously convenient hole in the bottom of the fence, and out into that oh so different territory, which was normally just the neighbour's gardens and the local park, but now was a wholly alien landscape. Cassivellaunus and Davidillidallion strode with confidence across the darkening lawns and through the flower beds, and I followed as best I could, feeling a bit like a tourist in the woods with an expert guide. I knew from the sky that we were heading South and West, but lost all other sense of direction, so that when we arrived in more open country with a hilly landscape and copses of trees, I had no idea where I was. On reflection, this was probably deliberate policy on their part, because what they were about to reveal was something which had been kept carefully concealed for a long time.

They approached a particular hillock with a lot of care, looking around and throwing glances back over their shoulders from time to time. We stopped at the foot of the hill by a little clump of hawthorn, and Davi said, "Please would you look away now, Mr Geoff, this part is very private." I stood with my back to them admiring the lights of outer London in the distance and trying to get my bearings, until Davi declared. "You can look now!" and I turned to see that they were waiting at a little wooden door which had materialised in the depths of the hawthorns.

It was a heavily studded, solid little door, small even by their standards, and I could have sworn that it wasn't there when I had looked before. Doubtless it was hidden from most eyes by assorted spells and curses, so I did feel quite privileged as Cassivellaunus swung it open and crouched through it. He fumbled about in the dark for twig torches and a fire-steel, finally handing a blazing torch each to Davi and I and taking one himself.

We headed down a narrow earth corridor with Cass leading and me as the rear-guard, the blazing torches flickering fitfully and our shadows leaping crazily on the walls.

The corridor opened into a small earthen cave, and I was suitably impressed by what I saw there. Piled from floor to ceiling was more silver than you could shake a stick at, in every form imaginable. There were cups and chalices, some dented and tarnished and some bright and perfect. there were chains and pendants, necklaces and dishes, crucifixes, swords sheathed and hilted with silver, and even a solid silver teddy bear sitting on top of the heap. I stood open mouthed, and goggle eyed as the torchlight flickered over this unspeakable fortune.

Cassivellaunus eventually broke the spell when he said, "That's just the silver, gold's in the next room."

We progressed through another tunnel, waving the acrid torch smoke away from our faces, and emerged into a slightly smaller cave which was, if anything, more splendid still. This was indeed where the gold was. Frighteningly large volumes of gold, again in every format imaginable, from gold covered books to torcs and bracelets, bowls and goblets, and even a crown or two, I noticed. Again, the three of us stood for a while just drinking it in.

This time it was Davidillidallion who said, "Jewels and other sundry valuables are in the third chamber, but we probably don't need to look at those too."

I followed them back to the doorway in a somewhat stunned state, and once outside again I stood in the darkened woodland with my back turned, while they cast whatever spells and curses protected that huge metallic fortune. We began the homeward journey in thoughtful silence, but I eventually managed to say, "I think you have more than sufficient funds for our woodland project, gentlemen. How can we convert it into useable cash, though? You'll need about £20,000 in men's money, maybe a little less, depending on the size of the wood and where it is."

Cassivellaunus looked at Davi and replied, "Shouldn't be a problem, Mr Geoff, we've used a broker before, he's of the folk, but he understands men's transactions and he has connections. You'd be surprised! If you can find the right woods, we'll go and take a look, then approach him about making some of our hoard available to buy it."

I nodded at this, it sounded totally reasonable, I had to admit. "How did you accumulate such an impressive, er, hoard?" I asked.

Cass smiled at this. "We've been carpenters and joiners for a long, long time, Mr Geoff," he said. "We've made pieces for kings and nobles, everyday furniture for ordinary folk and special projects too, from time to time. We've been doing it for much longer than you've been in the world, no offence, and we've accumulated some savings over the centuries. All the fruits of honest labour and fine skills though," he added, a bit defensively. "We've never raided or pillaged for any of it. Oh no." Again, I nodded and said I was pleased to hear it. We continued on our way in silence, and I said my farewells at the summer house before reverting to man-size and heading indoors for the night. Tomorrow I'd start to buy a little wood somewhere!

18. Done Deal

Early next morning I got online and started searching for 'woods for sale.' One or two looked OK, except that they were too big, too small, or too near a town. Eventually I hit on a little wood, about one and a half acres, called Kettle Wood. It was mixed ash and beech and had a brook running through one edge, and to me it looked pretty much perfect. It was in Hertfordshire, which certainly put it within easy driving distance, although it was probably quite a trek across several kingdoms by hedgehog. I considered showing the website to Cassivellaunus and Davidillidallion but thought better of it. I could see all sorts of complications.

Probably the best bet would be to arrange a viewing and smuggle them along with me in the back of the car. Disappearing into the woods was pretty much their forte after all, so I didn't think there would be any problem with engineering a good look around for them. I bit the bullet and called the agents straight away, and they turned out to be really helpful. By the time I went to tell the lads, we had a viewing arranged for the following

Wednesday, meeting the agent in the lane adjoining Kettle Wood at ten thirty a.m.

Cassivellaunus and Davidillidallion were very enthusiastic, thank goodness, and wanted to know much more about Kettle Wood than I could tell them, but decided they could just about wait until Wednesday to go and see for themselves. On the day, I put a few essentials in the car, leaving my coat on the back seat so as to have an excuse to leave the rear door open for the lads to escape into the woods. We drove the M1 Northward into Hertfordshire, Cass and Davi utterly astonished by the weight of traffic on the road, and then followed minor roads to Kettle Wood.

I'd arrived early as usual, so it was no problem to park on the access lane and let the lads loose, under a strict injunction to return when I sounded the horn twice. Mr Atkins, the agent, arrived promptly at ten thirty and we talked for a while standing by the cars. I explained that some friends and I were considering buying the wood as an investment, and as a centre for our wood carving and furniture interests, and he thought Kettle Wood was ideal for our purposes, being small and self-contained, but with some good mature trees as well as some coppiced stock. We headed into the trees along the muddy track, and he explained which trees predominated, and also pointed out the little brook at the bottom corner of the plot, *a beautiful feature in its own right*, I thought.

We headed back to the cars having agreed that I'd contact him the next morning with a firm decision, having discussed it with my friends, and I let him turn his car around and get back onto the road before I sounded the horn to call Cassivellaunus and Davidillidallion back to the car. They were both very positive and said it was a small wood with good timber and a really good feeling about it.

Apparently, some of the trees were quite ancient, and most were very welcoming, and there were lots of good spots for building a workshop and a home. They agreed with me that the brook was an excellent feature, and furthermore said it had a really nice character. Apparently, it was the sort of brook you could get along with. As we wended our way back to the M1 I explained that I'd arranged to call Mr Atkins the following day with a decision, at which point Cassivellaunus announced, "I think we're decided, actually. It's a great opportunity and it will be a break from all that happened in the Brent valley, our banishment, the feud with Balker, Guthrum's thugs and all of that. We'll talk to our broker tomorrow and arrange to convert some of our hoard into man's money, and if you don't mind, could you call the agent and tell him it's a deal? Tell him we'll pay the asking price, fair and square."

I nodded to them in the rear-view mirror and said, "So long as you're sure, we'll get the deal done tomorrow. Good. Bear in mind I can't offer Mr Atkins a chest of silver and a couple of gold crowns though!"

Cassivellaunus smiled at this and said, "I was thinking of a BACS payment to your account actually, Mr Geoff. I'll just need the account number and sort code." When we got home, I wrote the details on a little post-it note for Cass, then headed indoors to tell Lorraine and Linda that I'd seen the woods in question, that our carving group had decided to buy it, and that I'd invest £2000 from my savings bond as my share.

"Summer picnics in the woods!" I said. "Camping under the stars!" The picnics were better received than the camping, I think.

"At least you'll have somewhere to go and generate piles of wood chip without walking it through the house," commented Lorraine. "Plus, we'll own our own land—we'll have an estate!"

"A very small one, yes." I confirmed.

Things moved quite quickly after that. Cassivellaunus confirmed that his broker had transferred the funds to my account, I arranged with Mr Atkins to pay the asking price and to go to his office to sign the deeds, and by the end of the following week he confirmed that the land was now registered in the names of Cassivellaunus,

Hollyfoot and Denman. I sat on the summer house veranda that evening with Cassivellaunus and Davidillidallion, and a bowl of finest old *Cat's Eye* mead, and we drank a toast, 'to Kettle Wood, and to new beginnings'.

"I expect it's called Kettle Wood after the name of some previous owner." I hazarded. "Reginald Kettle, Ferdinand Kettle. Something like that."

Davi smiled up at me a bit indulgently I thought, and said, "Actually, Mr Geoff, it's in the *shape* of a kettle. An old beech told me. That's why it's always been Kettle Wood. And we're going to make it our home, and the heart of a whole new business, starting tomorrow. Cheers!"

19. Homecoming

We discussed plans for moving Cassivellaunus and Davidillidallion from the summer house to Kettle Wood. I mistakenly thought this would be a straightforward matter of loading the contents of the workshop into the boot of my car and dropping them off in Hertfordshire, but apparently not. Cassivellaunus patiently explained to me that first he and Davi would be obliged to visit everyone they knew in the Brent Valley, customers and suppliers as well as friends, take them a leaving gift and formally say their farewells. It seemed this would take a couple of weeks, minimum.

After that, the tools and materials in the workshop would need to go into safe storage somewhere, along with all their household possessions, while they undid all the spells which somehow kept the workshop floating in its interdimensional space, and so decommission it once and for all. When that was done, they could finally move all their possessions to the woods and set about building a new home and workshop.

Ironically, this part of the plan didn't seem to faze either of them at all.

It seemed that a week or two camping in the woods with your worldly goods around you was the most natural thing in the world. I suggested that they could use the secret back-up workshop which they'd squirrelled away behind my shed as a storage space, but they explained that this would have to be decommissioned too, in case any other magical being detected its aura and moved in, apparently. All rather worrying. In the end it was agreed that I'd leave two large storage boxes in the shed where I had my own workshop, and that they would gradually fill them as they moved things out. That would also make it easier to load up the car when the time came. They had at least accepted a lift over to Kettle Wood, which was good news.

And so Cassivellaunus and Davidillidallion entered into a long round of social calls and receiving guests. I spotted Mistresses Catalina and Meg calling at the workshop, and Thorfinn and Martin, although thankfully *not* Master Feller Bellerkind. The lads were often not to be found at the bottom of the garden, and I imagined them on a long perambulation of the Brent valley, visiting everyone (and probably every*thing*) they'd ever had dealings with. I checked on the storage boxes most days, and noted that they were gradually filling with tools, and with what I presumed to be the lad's own furniture, which was surprisingly modest and ordinary for two master crafts folk.

Eventually the day came when I was in the garden and heard Davidillidallion hissing to me from under the birdbath to get my attention. We headed down to the summer house where we could sit together a bit less conspicuously, and Cassivellaunus joined us on the veranda.

"I think we're finally ready for the move, Mr Geoff," he announced. "All our worldly goods are packed in your huge boxes, we've said our farewells to everyone we need to, and made our workshops here safe so that you don't have to worry about goblins and such like after we've gone. When would it be a good time to take us to Kettle Wood, I wonder?" I had a think and suggested the day after tomorrow, which seemed to suit everyone, so we arranged to meet at the car at ten thirty a.m. I'd load up the boxes beforehand, so we should be able to simply belt up and go (or in their case sit craning their necks on the back-seat bleachers, quite oblivious to seat belts).

The fateful morning arrived, and I made my excuses about meeting my friends at the woods (which was not entirely untrue) and headed out to the car. Cassivellaunus and Davidillidallion appeared out of the roses as I approached and were quickly installed in the rear foot wells, waiting for the all-clear to clamber onto their bench, once we were under way. They were becoming seasoned motorists. As we wended our way towards Staples Corner and the start of the M1 it occurred to me that they were leaving their home of many years, and their circle of friends, for a wholly new life.

"Are you both feeling OK?" I asked. "I know this is a big upheaval for you both, and quite a challenge."

Cassivellaunus smiled back at me in the rear-view mirror. "It's the best thing we've done in years, Mr Geoff. We've both learned the value of living among trees in these past days, and our old home holds mixed memories, bad and good both. When we've settled in, we'll invite everyone to a feast to celebrate our new beginning. You too, of course." *A housewarming party in the woods*, I thought, *novel*!

Soon enough we arrived at Kettle Wood and found it blessedly quiet. I was able to park pretty much at the gate in the lane, and we stepped out of the car into the wonderful embrace of bird song and that leafy woodland smell. I had wondered how Cass and Davi planned to move everything to their new home, and indeed what their new home was. No doubt all would become clear. It turned out that a good old-fashioned wheelbarrow provided the transport, although I carried a fair volume of their worldly belongings in one of the storage boxes. We hiked through the woods to a very old and stumpy yew, where they stopped, and I stood around expectantly.

"This is it, then?" I queried, a bit hesitantly.

Cassivellaunus nodded. "With a little everyday magic this old hollow yew will make a perfectly comfortable home for us to start out with," he explained. "We've got our eye on a little hillock at the top end of the wood, where we plan to excavate a workshop and a permanent home and make it really comfortable. The Folk were known as 'the people under the hill' before we were 'the fairies at the bottom of the garden', you know!"

Nothing surprised me any more, so I just put down the box next to the yew stump and said, "I'll go back for the rest."

Removals

Soon enough everything was unloaded, and it seemed like time to say goodbye.

"Is there anything else I can do to help out?" I asked. "I can lend you my golf umbrella from the car if you like, and maybe the waterproof ground sheet that I keep in the boot?"

Cassivellaunus smiled up at me a bit indulgently I thought, and replied, "No, thank you, Mr Geoff. We're perfectly able to set up a comfortable shelter for tonight and start on something more permanent tomorrow. Our folk have been coping outside quite a lot longer than yours, after all!" *Fair point*, I thought. They probably knew exactly what they were doing and were doubtless waiting for me to go away so that they could do it.

"We'll send a crow and let you know how things are going," said Davi. "As soon as we've got things around a bit, we'll ask you over to visit. Please don't worry though, we're more than content here."

Cassivellaunus nodded his agreement. "Travel safely on that mad road, Mr Geoff." He said. "We'll see you soon."

I waved my farewells, wished them luck and set off down the track between the trees to where the car was waiting. It felt like the day when I dropped off my son at university to start his first term! I consoled myself with the thought that if anyone could live comfortably in the woods, those two could.

Back at home things felt a bit numb. I hadn't realised before that the summer house and my own workshop had been bathed in a bit of a magical aura, I suppose, but now they were totally ordinary. It was all a bit depressing. I prinked about in the garden and did all the routine late Spring stuff, but I knew that really, I was waiting for a crow to caw for my attention. The caw finally came one morning while I was tinkering in my workshop, and I was able to furtively relieve the bird of his burden and reward him with a meaty treat before taking the message cylinder back inside. It was quite a long message, so I found my magnifying glass and read:

Dear Mr Geoff,

Greetings from your friends in Kettle Wood. We both thought we should let you know how things are going, as you were plainly worried about our welfare (quite needlessly)! We have made a very comfortable shelter in the old yew stump, using a few basic spells, and have moved all our belongings under cover. The weather has been changeable but not terrible, so we have made a good start on our permanent home and workshop. We have enlisted the help of Thorfinn Thorfinnson and Martin who are both good engineers, and together we have already excavated the main rooms.

The woods themselves are really, very welcoming. No members of the folk have lived here for a great many years, but we have introduced ourselves to all the older trees and have been very graciously received. There are of course men who walk through the woods with their dogs occasionally, but not to any troublesome extent. The stream in the woods is good, sweet water and the hunting is good too, so we shall certainly not go hungry. We had an excellent spit-roasted squirrel with Thorfinn and Martin after we had completed the main diggings, and they agreed it was the best they had ever tasted. Very nutty.

We sincerely hope you are coping without our company and finding plenty to keep you occupied. We shall write again when our permanent home is finished (probably around midsummer) and invite you to visit us.

Best wishes, Your friends

Cassivellaunus and Davidillidallion Hollyfoot.

It really was good to hear from them, I realised. I was so relieved that all was going well and that they weren't regretting their move. I decided I'd try to put them out of my mind for a while, get on with human life, and patiently await their next missive. I waited most of the summer as it happened and didn't hear from then again until the end of August when a crow cawed insistently at me until I got the message, literally and metaphorically. In the privacy of my workshop, I un-scrolled the letter and read the following:

Dear Mr Geoff,

Greetings from Cassivellaunus and Davidillidallion Hollyfoot, in Kettle Wood. We both apologise for not having written to you sooner, but our excuse is that we have been extremely busy, although only in a good way. The workshop and living quarters are now finished, and very splendid they are too, in our humble opinion! We plan to hold a celebratory party on the next full moon, with our closest friends from the Brent valley and would very much like you to come. Please reply by crow so that we can calculate how many guests to hunt for.

Very best wishes

Cassivellaunus and Davidillidallion Hollyfoot

I read over it again, then went to fetch my diary to see when the next full moon fell. The date was fine for me, so I mulled over excuses about badger watching at Kettle Woods, while I fetched pen and paper to write my acceptance note. When I was happy with it, I rolled it into the same small cylinder which the crow had brought and went to the fridge to find a sausage or something similar. Armed with a suitable meaty lure I laid out my runes on the grass and waited. Pretty soon a glossy black bird circled, landed, and waddled up to me, clearly familiar with the procedure. I showed him the treat, crouched as low as I could manage to make myself smaller, and very slowly extended my hands to tie the cylinder to his leg.

"Cassivellaunus and Davidillidallion Hollyfoot in Kettle Wood." I said, very clearly, then handed over the goodies, and he was gone.

The day finally came around and I got ready for my 'badger watching' expedition. I'd bought a bottle of Tawney Port as a gift, since you don't see *'Old Cat's Eye'* in the supermarket. I told Lorraine I'd be back before midnight and set off for the woods just before dusk, knowing that virtually all proceedings involving the folk began at that charged and magical time of day. It was quite dark by the time I arrived, but I parked up and found my way into the woods with no problems before I realised that I had no idea of where in Kettle Wood Cass and Davi's new home was. I didn't much fancy stumbling round the whole one and a half acres looking for it, but I needn't have worried.

Davidillidallion had clearly been waiting for me and now he stepped out onto the path and gave me a very polite little bow. "Greetings, Mr Geoff!"

he began, "please join us to celebrate our homecoming." As he said this, I realised I was effortlessly his height, and the woods seemed suddenly wholly different, not frightening but certainly vibrant with life, with furtive activity in the bushes. The rising full moon lit the path quite well, and we easily made our way through the woods, heading uphill until we reached the hillock where they had made their home.

It was not as I had expected. Probably the fact that Davi had welcomed me and subtly tuned me in to his world had altered my perceptions, but I saw it as a house rather than a hole in the hill. It had a veranda with steps and railings, all rather beautifully done, as you would expect from two master crafts folk. There was a varnished wooden front door in the centre with windows either side, and a hanging sign directing visitors to the workshop at the side.

"I'll show you round," said Davi and held the door open for me.

Inside it was quite spacious, with a central fireplace and two armchairs, a bookcase and a long case clock. It had something of the feel of a gentlemen's club, with dark wainscotting and an impressive candelabra in the centre of the ceiling. Through the short corridor at the back of the room were bedrooms and a kitchen, each lit by windows cut in the side of the hill. I could see now why the size and shape of the hillock was relevant, they had virtually hollowed out the crown of it. We went back outside through a smaller door at the rear of the house, and found Cassivellaunus, Mistresses Catalina and Meg, and Finnbar and Martin sitting around a fire, chatting, eating and drinking together. Cassivellaunus jumped up to greet me and show me to a seat by the fire, and I presented him with my bottle of port.

"It's not finest old *Cats Eye*," I said, "but it should hit the spot! Congratulations—you've created a truly beautiful home, not at all what I expected to find deep in the woods."

He smiled back and thanked me. "You're very welcome to visit us whenever you please, Mr Geoff," he said. "You know everyone here, so sit down and have some squirrel." I noticed several spitted specimens roasting over embers off to the side, it looked like the said squirrel, a rabbit and maybe a pigeon, so at least there were no horrors! To be honest the squirrel was really good, it actually was quite nutty!

Mistresses Catalina and Meg were well and delighted to be visiting Cass and Davi's new home, "So much more elegant than your old summer house, no offence intended," commented Mistress Catalina.

"Why, none taken," I responded. "Cassivellaunus and Davidillidallion have done a really professional job here. And I understand you both had a hand in it?" I asked, turning to Finnbar and Martin.

"Only the leg work, Mr Geoff," said Finnbar. They needed a lot of rooms dug and a lot of soil shifted, but you're right, they've made a really good hand of it." I raised my wooden cup of mead (only the one, because I was driving home when I was big enough to get into the car again).

"Here's to Cassivellaunus and Davidillidallion, and their new home in Kettle Wood," I proposed.

"Kettle Wood," they responded, and we all drank the most sincere toast to two beings who had become the closest friends to me.

I said my farewells when the full moon was high overhead, and the fire was dying down. I didn't know what the time was but it felt late, and I had a motorway drive ahead of me. Everyone wished me well, and Cassivellaunus and Davidillidallion escorted me down the track through the woods to where my car was waiting, my stature gradually returning to normal as we walked.

"Seriously, both of you, it's a lovely home, and I think life here in Kettle Woods must be perfect. I'll certainly be dropping by pretty regularly, and bringing Lorraine and Linda with me, mark my words!" Cassivellaunus' face was shadowed, but I knew he was smiling broadly.

"You do that, Mr Geoff," he said, "and remember, if ever you need anything making, there's no job too small."

'Bread Recipe.

Makes one loaf, or two small loaves, or eight *very* small loaves.

Requires:

500 grammes of strong white bread flour

One and a half teaspoons of fast acting dried yeast

1 teaspoon salt

300 millilitres of water

50 millilitres of olive oil.

Mix all the dry ingredients then add the oil and water. stir it all together until it forms a dough, then tip it out onto a flat surface for kneading.

Knead the dough for ten minutes. This entails ramming the ball of your hands into it to squash it, then rolling it round to squash it some more. This part is hard work, but it is necessary to build up gluten strands in the dough. It gets easier after this. It should start to feel smoother and less sticky as you knead.

After ten minutes kneading, oil a large bowl and put the dough in it. Cover it with a damp tea towel and leave it to rise for ninety minutes. It doesn't need to be in a really warm place. Normal kitchen temperature is fine.

After ninety minutes it will have risen to about double its original size. Tip it out and gently flatten it into a giant pancake. This is called 'knocking back' and removes all the gases which have built up in the gluten, which you encouraged by kneading.

'Form' the loaf, in other words give it its final shape. I fold two sides of the pancake into the middle then fold the whole thing in half lengthwise. I then roll it up tightly, like a Swiss roll, to squeeze any air out. I end up with a blunt ended cylinder. The layers you have made in the loaf by folding will help it to rise again and give it structural strength.

Put it on a baking sheet and cover with a damp tea towel, held up off of the loaf by some sort of contrivance. I use a microwave rack, but a couple of tin cans at each corner can work. The loaf has to prove that it has enough active yeast to rise again. This is 'proving' the loaf.

After an hour of proving, heat the oven to 200 degrees centigrade. Cut four or five diagonal slashes in the top of the loaf. This will allow the crust to open up as the loaf rises some more in the hot oven.

Bake for thirty or thirty five minutes in the middle of the oven. Ovens differ, so it might need a little longer or a little less. I tend to give it fifteen minutes on one side then turn it round to cook the other side for the last fifteen minutes, otherwise the fan assisted oven tends to burn the crust. You may also need to move it nearer the base of the oven if it bakes too violently in the middle.

Take it out and tap it on the bottom. If it sounds hollow, it's baked. If not give it a little longer. Put it on a wire rack to cool. It continues cooking and losing moisture as it cools, so wait until its fully cold before you store it (or eat it).

That's it! Enjoy.'